LETTERS FROM
PERVERSE UNIVERSITY
The Subversion of America
2nd Edition

Letters from Perverse University

Copyright © 2022 by *L. James Harvey Ph.D.*

Published in the United States of America
ISBN   Paperback: 978-1-958030-47-9
ISBN   eBook: 978-1-958030-48-6

All rights reserved. No part of this publication may be reproduced, stored in a retrieval system or transmitted in any way by any means, electronic, mechanical, photocopy, recording or otherwise without the prior permission of the author except as provided by USA copyright law.

The opinions expressed by the author are not necessarily those of ReadersMagnet, LLC.

ReadersMagnet, LLC
10620 Treena Street, Suite 230 | San Diego, California, 92131 USA
1.619. 354. 2643 | www.readersmagnet.com

Book design copyright © 2022 by ReadersMagnet, LLC. All rights reserved.

Cover design by *Kent Gabutin*
Interior design by *Ched Celiz*

LETTERS FROM PERVERSE UNIVERSITY

The Subversion of America
2nd Edition

L. James Harvey Ph.D.

ReadersMagnet, LLC

Dedication

This book is gratefully dedicated to those wonderful individuals who have been courageously fighting in America's Culture War. To those who have been unwilling to surrender the values upon which this country was founded and who have been fighting to preserve the history and heritage of the greatest country mankind has ever built. I applaud you and thank you for resisting the wokism, cancel culture, and socialist/Marxist forces which seek to destroy America so they can supposedly create a socialist utopia on the ruins of American democracy and capitalism. They will fail as have their fore runners who have tried the same devious methods in Russia, Cuba, Venezuela, and numerous other places. Their promised utopia inevitably leaves a depressed people and their promises become only a pile of ashes. I pray we might escape that fate.

Contents

Dedication v
Book Endorsements x
Preface xiii
Introduction xvii

Supreme Deception 1
Climate Change 3
Inflategate 6
Obama and Christianity 9
Trump Trump! 12
Gender Disruption 15
Paul Harvey Revisited 18
Evolution Emergency 21
Lowering Higher Education 23
Abortion Demise 26
Our Democrat Success 28
Support Soros 31
The Prager List 33
Bureaucratic Bliss 36
Euphemism Sunday 38
Pornography 40
Push Muslim Immigration! 43
Obama/Trump Hypocrisy Award 46
Antisemitism 48
Destroying the Family 51
Ride Antifa 53
Revolutionary Abolitionist Movement (Antifa) 54

The Biden Lies	56
Flag Desecration	59
Kill Freedom of Speech	61
The Unholy Alliance	64
Diversity Deception	67
Don't Kill Faith Delude It!	70
The Language Divide	73
Wonderful Obesity	75
American Successes	77
Kill Congressional Reform	80
The Fluke Incident	82
The Bisexual Time Bomb	84
Our 1619 Project	86
Kill the Military	90
Hyphenate America!	93
The "Me" Generation	95
Go Secularism!	97
American Betrayal	100
Censorship	103
Killing America Recap	105
Bless the APA	109
Keep Blacks Democrat	111
Push Hard Left	113
The Great Deception	116
The Feminization of America	118
Flag Desecration	121
The LOVE Trap	123
The Cake Court Cases	126
Kill Christianity	128
Killing Christians	131
How to Kill a Christian	132
Father Satan's Lecture	134
Destroy America Conference	137

Media Madness	140
Kill Charter Schools, Home Schooling, and Vouchers	142
Ride Wokism Kill Loudounism	145
Dead Churches	148
Kill Easter	150
The Solomon Solution	152
Temptation 101	154
The "Iron Triangle" Works!	156
Use the White Robes!	158
Societal Suicide	160
Hi-Tech Immorality	163
The Flower Lady	165
The Debt Killer	167
World View	170
Kill the Best	173
Open Borders	176
Laziness	178
Lecture on Roman Demise	180
Postscript	183
Other Book Titles From Dr. Harvey	190
Index	191

Book Endorsements

For those of us who read (maybe years ago) **The Screwtape Letters** by C.S. Lewis, and who thought we would never read a book like it, I have good news for you, Dr. L. James Harvey, who counts The Screwtape Letters, after the Bible, as one of the two works which have been instrumental in his intellectual adventure through life, gives to us **Letters From Perverse University** a very interesting way to look at issues we are facing today from a Christian viewpoint.

Dr. Harvey is a proven writer who has a good command, not only of the English language, but of how to deal with profound social issues. He is an avid reader whose research reaches into many topics that most of us are not even aware of.

In The Letters From Perverse University**,** you will discover Dr. Harvey's satirical treatment of issues like pornography, gender disruption, freedom of speech, the bisexual time bomb, climate change, Antifa, and many other topics. So, grab your book and sit down for an enlightened journey filled with true and factual information that is presented in a variety of ways —sometimes humorous—sometimes biting—but always true to what is taking place in contemporary American society.

—**Dr. Samuel Vinton, President Emeritus**
Grace Christian University,
Grand Rapids, Michigan

In a day when the church is neglected, Christianity is rejected, and Bible reading has radically declined (World Religious News indicates to 20%), AND at the same time eastern religions and Islam are increasing in our secularized society, there is a great need for discernment and insight into the underlying goal of "Satan" and "evil" in civilization from a truthful Biblical-Christian perspective. **"Letters From Perverse University"** gives a thought-provoking introduction, providing insight into the world of pagan thinking, mind-control, demonism, and deterioration of morals and values in our society.

—**Rev. Thomas Couch**
Senior Pastor, Grandville Bible Church
Grandville Michigan

* * *

Since attending the same high school together, many years ago, it has been so rewarding to find my life connected again to "Jim" Harvey. Dr. Harvey has successfully stepped up the educational ladder, position by position, always serving and contributing to the betterment of the many young people he was honored to serve.

From high school coaching, semi-pro and college sports, all the while pursuing advanced degrees, he soon found himself sought after as college dean, vice president, and president of institutions of higher learning. Each of these responsibilities, while requiring Jim to share his God given truths, proved to be a source of new knowledge and skills at every level to be added for the benefit of newer audiences.

Blessed by the love and longevity of life, Dr. Harvey's interest in being equipped with spiritual truth and discernment, has led to the marvelous "Letters From Perverse University." His hands-on knowledge of the educational systems, once the envy of the world, is absolutely necessary for today.

The pages of these remarkable letters, will turn by themselves, as the reader grasps the catastrophic purpose of errant educators, politicians, and leaders of today. Suspense, a bit of humor in the characters, and the plots and conflicts arising, will keep the pages turning. I think even C.S. Lewis would take note.

—**Robert (Bob) Azkoul**
Founder Director, Alpha Omega Ministries,
Music, Bible Distributors.
Grand Rapids, Michigan

* * *

May I introduce you to a wordsmith, a craftsman of exceptional talent who will not only open your mind but will also provide surprising food for thought?! Satan is at work, yes, but you will now view the underside as seen from an "insider" giving you the low-down so you will now have the upper-hand. Share what you read and your friends will marvel at your new found wit and wisdom. Just say "thanks", and tell them you have been feasting on Jim Harvey's new book.

Bon Appetite my friend!

—**Rev. Bill Campbell (retired).**
Wesleyan Church

* * *

This book on Letters From Perverse University will open your mind to the fact Satan is real and is out to influence the world. The Devil is a deceiver and will do all he can to cause the Christian to doubt his faith in Christ. These Letters will show you how Satan operates that could affect your life.

—**Rev. Douglas Wood**
Visitation Pastor, Grandville Bible Church
Grandville, Michigan

Preface

After the Bible, two books that standout as having a major impact on me in my intellectual journey through life have been, "The Screwtape Letters" (1) by C.S. Lewis and, "The Lessons of History" (2) by Will and Ariel Durant. C.S. Lewis, the eminent English scholar and writer, who was a convert to Christianity in later life and became a preeminent apologist for the faith, turned me on to the literary device called satire as well as to a deeper understanding of my faith in his book "Mere Christianity." Will and Ariel Durant's book was a succinct summary of what they had learned about history from studying and writing several volumes, 10 in all, about various periods of world history.

So, what do these two books have in common? They both take the position that there are forces of evil at work in the world. C.S. Lewis posits a devil who is tempting a person away from their faith in a satirical masterpiece, while Will and Ariel Durant, who were both avowed agnostics religiously, stated, "If history supports any theology this would be a dualism, a good spirit and an evil spirit battling for control of the universe and men's souls." (2:47).

C.S. Lewis said he was asked most often, after "The Screwtape Letters" became very popular, whether he really believed there was a devil (1:iv). He answered with a, "yes." He went on to say he accepted the traditional Christian position, as found biblically in Isaiah 14:12-17, Revelation 12:4-9, Ephesians 6:12 and other places, that Satan is really a fallen angel named Lucifer, who used his free will to rebel against God, and was cast out of heaven with 1/3 of the angels, who followed him in his rebellion. According to scripture, Satan and his followers inhabit the earth and are in conflict with God's forces for the hearts and lives of earth dwellers. We read in II Corinthians 11:14-15 ".... for Satan himself masquerades as an angel of light. It is not surprising then, if his servants masquerade as servants of righteousness. Their end will be what their actions deserve." (Bible New International Version)

As a history major in college, I became aware of the significant historical work of the Durant's and found it interesting that after that amount of study, from an objective and agnostic world view, they would reach a similar conclusion to that of C.S. Lewis, namely that the history of mankind reflects a conflict between good and evil here on earth.

Another author this writer came to appreciate deeply was Paul Tournier. He was a world renown Swiss psychiatrist whose books, "Guilt and Grace," "The Whole Person," and "The Strong and the Weak," gained a world-wide readership. In his book "The Person Reborn," Tournier says, "I believe in the existence of Satan, that is to say an active force for evil, infinitely cunning and capable of strategic plans. I believe there is a battle going on in the heart of every one of us between God and Satan. Both combatantants use the same psychological laws, such as the law of suggestion, which science studies, and which God created for good only. Let us beware of suggestions that come from the devil. As the old proverb says, 'he must have a long spoon that sups with the devil.' Let us beware of the suggestions that come from our own egotistical desires, our aggressiveness, our covetousness, and all those mechanisms of the unconscious that the devil handles with such skill." (3:159). So, says a brilliant psychiatrist.

It seems to the writer that even a cursory view of modern history reveals evil at work in the world. Hitler and the holocaust, Idi Amin and the murder of 300,000 of his countrymen, Pol Pot who killed close to 2 million Cambodians, Mao Zedong responsible for the deaths of over 50 million Chinese, Joseph Stalin for 23 million deaths, and we had the Hutus slaughtering the Tutsi in Africa, all demonstrate evil forces at work few can understand. Then we could talk about Charles Manson, Jim Jones, and the Church of Satan in San Francisco, which had 10,000 members, a "Satanic Bible" and which ultimately led to a mass suicide in South America.

We have also had a string of serial killers down through history whose destruction of innocent human life is hard to explain short of positing an evil force at work.

All down through history literature, art and the theater have reflected the belief in an evil spirit called the devil. Milton's "Paradise Lost" and Dante's "Inferno", and Goethe's "Faust" come to mind. Some of our more modern movies have also reflected this belief as evidenced by "Rosemary's Baby", "the Portrait of Dorian Grey", "The Exorcist", "The Omen", and "The Demon." The truth is most people believe there are evil forces at work in the world and believe they are organized and have a leader.

If we accept the fact there is an evil force with a leader named Satan, Lucifer, or something else (the Bible also uses Beelzebub, Mephistopheles, the Devil or just the Enemy to refer to this leader) then it makes sense for us to spend some time thinking about how this force or person operates and/or might affect us. I believe C.S. Lewis performed an important service in suggesting we should spend some time thinking about how such a force might think and operate. Any army or competitive group of any kind usually spends a great deal of time thinking about how their opposition might be operating in order to combat them more effectively. As a former high school coach, I remember how much time we spent learning all we could find out about what our prospective opponents were likely to do when we played them.

It simply makes sense for Christians to spend some time thinking about how Satan might be attacking them or trying to influence their behavior in a negative way. I also believe we should ask what forces might be at work to undermine and harm our nation.

Paul Tournier believes the way Satan and God compete for our souls is by putting thoughts in our minds and by relying on the forces of suggestion. We then, through the freedom God gave us to choose must make decisions. It is in choosing rightly that we please God and it is in making wrong choices that we harm ourselves and are drawn away from our maker. This book through the literary device of satire seeks to make the reader more aware of this process and how it impacts our nation as we face the 21st century.

Because of the greatness of "The Screwtape Letters" this writer was hesitant to even use a similar approach through satire, however, I choose to do so not out of any attempt to approach the brilliance of C.S. Lewis, but rather to say this vehicle for understanding evil is valid and one that Christians ought to employ more often. Anything we can do to expose evil can be helpful.

I have chosen, in this work, to focus on issues which are critical to our nation today. I truly believe our greatness as a nation is rooted in our founder's values and in the Judeo/Christian foundation upon which our basic documents and traditions are built. I also believe there are forces at work to take down our nation and move us and the world toward a global world government based on values that are secularist and atheistic at best. As Will and Ariel Durant have said, "There is no significant example in history, before our time, of a society successfully maintaining a moral life without the aid of religion" (2:50). There are, I believe, evil forces at work trying to undermine our faith and our values and they tend to operate best in the dark. To the extent that this book sheds some light on these forces it will be a success. Light always trumps darkness. Our nation's future depends to a large extent on the collective outcomes of the skirmishes and battles that are constantly being fought in our minds. I pray this book will aid sincere Americans in winning the majority of these battles. At the end of the book in the Post Script, the author will provide the reader with some suggestions on how to be victorious in these battles.

L. James Harvey Ph.D.

1. Lewis, C.S., "The Screwtape Letters." New York: The Macmillan Co. Macmillan Paper Back Edition, 11th printing, 1969.
2. Durant, Will and Ariel, "The Lessons of History", New York: Simon and Schuster, Sixth printing, 1966.
3. Tournier, Paul, "The Person Reborn". New York: Harper & Row Publishers, 1966.

Introduction

The Letters from Perverse University that follow are letters from a professor of Deception at Perverse University in Hell. Professor Luscious Academianut Ph.D. teaches Deception 101, Deception 201, and a Senior Seminar Deception 401. These courses along with the other courses the students take prepare them for service in countries around the world as they try to take down established governments creating chaos that inevitably leads to the people of the country inviting people working for the evil forces to take over the country in a dictatorship led by Satan. The ultimate objective is to create a world- wide global government, predicted in the Bible in the end times, that will be governed by Satan.

The following letters are letters regularly sent by the professor to his former students who are working in the USA to undermine the democratic capitalistic system based on Judeo/Christian principles which has become the world's super power. The letters instruct the students in how to carry out their activities in order to attain maximum results.

As you will see in the first letter below, I have found a way to get into the communications system P.U. set up with its students and I have discovered how to intercept their correspondence.

This book displays the Letters I have received and are presented so you the readers might better understand how our adversaries are operating.

Following is one of a series of letters intercepted by Dr. L. James Harvey. They are from a Professor of Deception at Perverse University in Hell and are sent to his former students who are in the U.S.A. working to tempt America away from its Judeo/Christian values. Dr. Harvey has edited the profanity out of the letters and presents them for your information.

Perverse **U**niversity ™

Department of Deception
P.O. Box 666
Smoke City, Hades 66666

Home of the Fighting Red Devils

Supreme Deception

Memo To: All Tempters Serving in the USA
From: Luscious Academianut Ph.D.
Regarding: Theft of Letters

It is my unhappy duty to advise you we have had a terrible breach of security here at Perverse University. One of my most trusted associates has betrayed our communications network to one of the Enemy's friends in the U.S.A. allowing him to capture the letters I have been sending you for some time.

What is worse this # $ % ^ & thief (pardon my language) is now, we believe, about to publish a large number of my personal letters and correspondence to you for all Americans to read. This horrid person is Dr. L. James Harvey. We have reason to believe this Dr. Harvey already has a publisher ready to publish a large portion of our confidential material. You must do everything you possibly can to prevent the publication of the material, and if you can, please get rid of this traitor Harvey. Father Satan is furious over this breech of security and if we can get our hands on the culprit he will be punished beyond belief.

I can't tell you how sorry I am this happened. We are now rethinking how we communicate with all of you and are looking at ways we can prevent it from happening again. We may even have to rethink our master plan. We'll let you know if that happens.

If you come across some of the letters in print deny that they are ours. Present them as the figment of some traitorous thoughts of one of the Enemy's people. Most Americans will probably forget rather soon that they exist and continue to go about their business.

We have the U.S.A. so far down our Father's "Slippery Slope" that we don't believe they can recover. Just keep up the good work and our ultimate victory is assured.

Following is one of a series of letters intercepted by Dr. L. James Harvey. They are from a Professor of Deception at Perverse University in Hell and are sent to his former students who are in the U.S.A. working to tempt America away from its Judeo/Christian values. Dr. Harvey has edited the profanity out of the letters and presents them for your information.

Perverse University ™

Department of Deception
P.O. Box 666
Smoke City, Hades 66666

Home of the Fighting Red Devils

Climate Change

Dear Sciencedown,

Our climate change program is in deep trouble. You've got to rescue it. It is critical to the support of our political efforts to destroy fossil fuels and the western economies based on these carbon-based elements. That horrid Whistle Blower magazine has published some of the failings of our supporters and you must counter attack them. Here are some of the things they published:

1. Al Gore said in 2008 that by the Summer of 2013 the Artic would-be ice free. It isn't.
2. The Associated Press reported in 1989 that by 2019 the West Side Highway in New York would be under water because of global warming and it isn't.
3. In 2009 Prince Charles in England said there were only 8 years left to save the planet.
4. The New York Time reported in 1970 that "pollution expert" James Lodge Jr. claimed a new ice age would be upon us by 2000. It isn't.
5. In 1970 NASA's S.I. Rasool insisted that over the next five to 10 years there would be such a temperature decrease it could trigger an ice age. It didn't.

6. In 2019 Ocasio-Cortez claimed that in just a few short years Miami would disappear because of global warming. She also said we only had 12 years left to save the planet.
7. In 1972 Brown University scientists wrote President Nixon stating that "very soon" world global climate would deteriorate at a magnitude never experienced by mankind. It hasn't.
8. In 1974 the London Guardian reported a new ice age was coming fast. It isn't.

Do you see our problems? Some of our scientists predict global warming and others an ice age. They can't both be right. But the greatest problem we have is that this Dr. Art Robinson, who is co-founder of the Linus Pauling Institute of Science and Medicine was instrumental in sending out a petition which was signed by 31,000 scientists worldwide (including over 9,000 with Ph.D.'s) which stated:

"There is no convincing scientific evidence that human release of carbon dioxide, methane, or other greenhouse gases is causing or will, in the foreseeable future, cause catastrophic heating of the Earth's climate. Moreover, there is substantial evidence that increases in atmospheric carbon dioxide produce many beneficial effects upon the natural plant and animal environments of the earth."

Do you see our problem? You must get some of our Democrat "scientists" to counter act this horrible attack on our pet project. We are counting on a Democrat win in November so our friends can begin their "Green Revolution" destroying the coal and oil industries in the U.S. Think about how many Americans will be unemployed and the disaster this will create in the American economy. This on top of the pandemic and its economic destruction will crush America and destroy it as a super power. Our Chinese friends await in the wings to destroy America economically by destroying the dollar as the world's reserve currency, and forcing America to bend to its will. China will support our communist and socialist friends in the Democrat Party who will take over in America and build toward that wonderful one world government that Father Satan will take over and rule the world. The Enemy will be finally defeated and all his supporters either killed or converted to our purposes.

We can win this but you've got to kill off those horrid scientific truth tellers that are hurting our climate change program.

Your Magnificent and Supremely Endowed Genius,

X

Luscious Academianut Ph.D.

P.S. Please keep our friends from blaming former President Trump for climate change. It doesn't pass the "smell test." Since the earth has been cooling and heating in cycles for thousands of years even idiots, like our followers, can figure out a president in office for four years couldn't cause global climate change. This will backfire on us. Stop it!

LETTERS FROM PERVERSE UNIVERSITY

Following is one of a series of letters intercepted by Dr. L. James Harvey. They are from a Professor of Deception at Perverse University in Hell and are sent to his former students who are in the U.S.A. working to tempt America away from its Judeo/Christian values. Dr. Harvey has edited the profanity out of the letters and presents them for your information.

Perverse University ™

Department of Deception
P.O. Box 666
Smoke City, Hades 66666

Home of the Fighting Red Devils

Inflategate

Dear Pound Foolish,

I can't tell you how proud we are of you and your devils for enticing the U.S. Congress to pass the new budget and spending bill. Our economists here at old P.U. believe this legislation may be the last hurdle before the U.S. economy runs into deep trouble. The bill, crafted by two of the most famous swamp creatures (Mitch McConnell and Chuck Schumer) eliminates all attempts to reign in Federal spending, destroys the promises the Republicans made to voters in the 2016 election, furthers wasteful social spending, could easily destroy the dollar, and increase inflation, which could undermine the economy. The budget and spending will add at least $1 trillion dollars to next year's debt and make 67 straight years where the U. S. Government has failed to pay down one cent on the national debt, which just hit $30 trillion. Spending projections make it likely the government could not possibly pay down on the debt in the next 10 years setting up certain financial disaster.

Since 1971, when President Nixon decoupled the dollar from gold the dollar has lost 95% of its value and it is about to go further down the drain. If inflation continues to go up as expected, the ability of the U.S. to finance its trillions of dollars of debt will go up and place the whole economy in danger, just as we have planned and predicted. The Federal Reserve will have to have its printing presses running 24 hours to produce enough dollars to pay interest on the debt, and each dollar will reduce the value of those already in circulation. This is the stuff which can birth riots and bring governments down, as we have caused in other countries in the past. Great work!

Fortunately, the idiot swamp creatures (read politicians of both parties) never paid attention to the last president to take the Federal debt seriously. The last to pay down on the debt was Dwight Eisenhower. He warned Americans about debt and the Military Industrial Complex (MIC), which he said could easily cause the debt to balloon. This happily occurred. The rampant corruption and cronyism in the MIC have American funding a military with planes it doesn't want, ships it can't use, and tanks for the last war, and a military budget of more than the military asked for. All of this while our two strongest enemies spend far less than the U.S. Russia spends 10% of what the U.S. does and China about 31% of the U.S. outlay. The U.S. pours billions into a Pentagon budget that wastes billions, has never been audited, though the law requires it, and funds 800,000 civilians (1 for every 2 service personnel). Billions of dollars have gone missing into the pockets of corrupt politicians, foreign dictators, and dishonest military contractors and their lobbyists, and yet a bankrupt nation throws more money at the MIC beast just as Eisenhower predicted could happen. Add to that President Biden's stupid exit from Afghanistan left $84 billion in new military hardware for the Islamic terrorists. Fortunately, no American president can do anything about the MIC mess because the power rests with the swamp creatures like McConnell, and Schumer and their numerous buddies on the take from lobbyists, military contractors, and major contributors to their campaigns.

Thankfully the Democrats made a budget deal to increase social spending, which wastes as much money as the MIC. We laughed down here when Obama doubled the national debt in 8 years and piled up more debt than every president before him combined. Over $10 trillion in debt America can never pay back. We rejoiced here at P.U. as Obama spent $800 billion on his stimulus plan, much of which went to cronies and green energy projects that went belly up, like Solyndra. His Obama phone project, which gave free iPhone to everyone on welfare was fantastic. We cheered as many recipients sold the phones for drug and alcohol money, and others used them to call friends to discuss when they would get their next food stamps and how they could get a good section 8 housing grant to allow them to live rent free in a nice crime free upper middleclass neighborhood.

Donald Trump didn't do much better in the spending. He significantly increased the military budget and then near the end of his four years was caught having to spend trillions to counter the covid-19 epidemic.

Now Biden is spending trillions the U.S.A. doesn't have on infrastructure and green climate projects for Democrat cronies. And the spending goes on and on until economic reality forces the U.S.A. into a financial disaster. Just what we want.

Those Americans never learn and fortunately not enough of them are currently committed to the Enemy and his horrid values to stop the insanity and drain the swamp. Full speed ahead we've got them on the ropes and your great work will certainly earn you a promotion when the U.S. collapses.

Your spectacularly brilliant professor,

X

Luscious Academianut Ph.D.

Following is one of a series of letters intercepted by Dr. L. James Harvey. They are from a Professor of Deception at Perverse University in Hell and are sent to his former students who are in the U.S.A. working to tempt America away from its Judeo/Christian values. Dr. Harvey has edited the profanity out of the letters and presents them for your information.

Perverse University ™

Department of Deception
P.O. Box 666
Smoke City, Hades 66666

Home of the Fighting Red Devils

Obama and Christianity

Dear Faithdown,

Father Satan recently gave a talk here at P.U. in which he shared with us some of the wonderful things we got the Obama Administration to do in the U.S. to damage Christianity while he was president. I'm sending you a list of some of the things so you can educate your soldiers about the kind of actions we would like to encourage leaders in the U.S.A. to take. Here is the list:

1. In 2009 Obama removed all religious elements from the White House Christmas cards. Instead, the cards reflected items on the White House Christmas tree ornaments like family dogs, and figurines like Mao Tso-Tung and a drag queen.

2. In 2009 the Obama administration shut out all pro-life groups from attending a White House sponsored health conference.

3. In a deliberate act of disrespect Obama nominated three pro-abortion ambassadors to the Vatican. The Vatican rejected all three.

4. While speaking at Georgetown University, Obama ordered that a monogram symbolizing Jesus' name be covered while he spoke.

5. Obama officials assembled a terrorism dictionary calling pro-life advocates violent and charging that they use racism in their "criminal" activities.

6. In 2009 Obama refused to host services for the National Day of Prayer at the White House. This day has been established by Federal law.

7. In 2009 Obama extended federal benefits to same sex partners of Foreign Service and Executive Branch employees. This violated the Defense of Marriage Act.

8. Obama deliberately began omitting the phrase "the creator" when quoting the Declaration of Independence. He did this repeatedly.

9. In 2010 Obama cut funding for 176 abstinence programs.

10. In 2011 Obama refused to allow a cross to be re-erected at a WWII memorial in the Mojave Desert even though a court had ordered the government to do so.

11. Obama avoided any religious references in his Thanksgiving speeches.

12. Obama opposed inclusion of President Roosevelt's famous D-Day Prayer in the WWII Memorial.

13. The Obama Administration forgave student loans for students in exchange for public service, but not if the student service was with a religious organization.

14. In 2013 Pastor Louie Giglio was removed from offering a prayer at the inauguration ceremony because he once preached a sermon supporting traditional marriage.

15. In 2014 Obama sought funding for every type of sex education except that which taught traditional moral values.

16. In 2011 Obama sought for the first time in history a non-discriminating law in hiring that did not protect religious freedom forcing religious groups to hire those who opposed their beliefs.

Isn't this a great list? And these aren't the only things Obama did to help destroy Christianity in the U.S. We need more presidents and followers like that and we'll take the U.S. down. That horrible motto "In God We Trust" will soon become "In God We Trusted" <GG>. Just add the "ed" and we got them!

Your Brilliant and Humble Professor,

Luscious Academianut Ph.D.

PS. Father Satan just became aware of a book in the U.S. and he's furious. He wants the book and author destroyed. The book is "Dark Agenda – The War to Destroy Christian America." The book lays bare all our strategies and attempts to destroy Christianity, including naming the people who have been helping us. Father Satan said if you allow that book to get on the New York Times best seller list you will be recalled and disciplined. Please do all you can to undermine the book and author David Horowitz. The worst part of this is, the book has been written by a Jew.

LETTERS FROM PERVERSE UNIVERSITY

Following is one of a series of letters intercepted by Dr. L. James Harvey. They are from a Professor of Deception at Perverse University in Hell and are sent to his former students who are in the U.S.A. working to tempt America away from its Judeo/Christian values. Dr. Harvey has edited the profanity out of the letters and presents them for your information.

Perverse University ™

Department of Deception
P.O. Box 666
Smoke City, Hades 66666

Home of the Fighting Red Devils

Trump Trump!

Dear Peopledown,

I'm writing to remind you of a problem we've had with the Enemy all down through history, which is repeating itself in the U.S. today. The problem is that the Enemy has the horrible habit of using people we have won to our values to accomplish his purposes. This tendency is driving our Father Satan to distraction. The Enemy has used murderers, adulterers, and even a prostitute to further his purposes. In ancient times he used Moses, David, Sampson, and Rahab, all deeply flawed people to serve him. These are people we thought we could count on because they all gave in to temptations, we thought put them on our side. Now, in the U.S. the Enemy is doing it again and it threatens many of our hard-earned gains. Warn all your colleagues of this devious behavior by the Enemy.

I'm, of course, referring primarily to the former president of the U.S. Donald Trump. Here's a man we thought we had won over and was in our camp. After all we tempted him with riches, got him to invest in and encourage gambling, led him into sexual excesses, including 2 divorces and 3 marriages, led him into 4 bankruptcies where he violated promises to compensate other businesses, and helped him develop a prideful ego of large proportions. You'd think after those successes we had we could count on him to serve our agenda and further our causes as the president. But he didn't. Now, he threatens a comeback and the traitor is likely to further the causes of the Enemy in the U.S. even more. You must stop him!

Behind our backs a man we thought was going to do our will has formed an allegiance with a large group of evangelical Christians and conservatives and he's following their agenda threatening to undo some of our greatest accomplishments. You must undermine him. He has appointed conservative judges, many of them committed to the Enemy, and he promoted religious freedom, which is undermining many of the gains our homosexual friends have made. He also appointed that horrid servant of the Enemy, Betsy DeVos Secretary of Education, and she worked to undermine the godless public schools, we tried so hard to throw the Enemy out of. She also promoted charter schools, and private schools that teach the Enemy's values. She even wanted students to take tax money with them to the schools of their choice, even to schools dedicated to the Enemy. If Trump returns, we'll get more of this. You've got to stop him. The public schools of America are our greatest hope for getting rid of the Enemy's influence in the country, we can't let the students escape our influence.

We just can't let the Enemy take a person we had worked so hard on to be one of us, and use him for his own purposes. It just isn't fair! You must Trump Trump or you'll be removed.

Your Brilliant and Precocious Professor,

X

Luscious Academianut Ph.D.

P.S.—You still may get some bad out of Trump for us if you use his bloated ego and sexual proclivities to our advantage. He's still a potential plus for us, if you can wean him away from those dreadful evangelicals. Use his penchant for using foul language and for tweeting to undermine his effectiveness and turn many of the Enemy's people off on him. See if you can use his sexual proclivities to destroy his marriage and further undermine his relationship with the fundamental Christians.

P.S. II—I thought you'd like to know we have just added a new Hall of Fame to the wall in the faculty lounge here at old P.U. We call it the Chappaquiddick Hall of Fame. It will contain the names of all the prominent American politicians who have been serial adulterers in the U.S.A. We've already added the names of Lyndon Johnson, John F. Kennedy, Bill Clinton, and Teddy Kennedy. We'd like to add Trump next – keep working on him.

Following is one of a series of letters intercepted by Dr. L. James Harvey. They are from a Professor of Deception at Perverse University in Hell and are sent to his former students who are in the U.S.A. working to tempt America away from its Judeo/Christian values. Dr. Harvey has edited the profanity out of the letters and presents them for your information.

Perverse University ™

Department of Deception
P.O. Box 666
Smoke City, Hades 66666

Home of the Fighting Red Devils

Gender Disruption

Dear Gender Down,

Father Satan is really pleased with the success you have had in confusing people's minds regarding gender. You are having wonderful success in destroying the Enemy's binary system of male and female, which we believe will help destroy the traditional family and confuse the male/female roles the Enemy intended for building strong families and societies. With the help of our LGBTQ friends and the trans gender community you are eroding people's faith in the Enemy's plan. Keep up the good work! Make our professors in the public colleges come to believe the binary system of the Enemy is an outdated Bible based system that needs to give way to our modern system of multigenderedness.

We rejoiced when we heard that Facebook will now allow people to identify themselves in over 50 genders beside male and female. Some lists of genders go as high as 76 and they are being added all the time. The principle you have established is brilliant, namely that an individual can determine whatever gender they happen to "feel" they are at the moment and, in fact, their gender can change from time to time depending on their feelings without regard to their chromosomes or sex organs. This allows for some wonderful opportunities to confuse people and even leads to conflict if someone addresses someone using a pronoun that they object to because it conflicts with their gender feelings at the moment.

As you know, there are some crazy academics who are now saying that new born babies should not be labeled male or female at birth but rather should be allowed to select their own sex around 4 or 5 years of age or when they may reach a maturity level that would let them decide which gender, they would like to be regardless of their biological sex and chromosomes at birth. You must encourage this movement which is trying to get those in charge of birth certificates to list the sex of the new born as U (unknown or undecided) or X (undetermined) on the birth certificate until the child has a chance to make their choice. This is a fantastic opportunity to undermine the Enemy's binary system and throw extreme confusion in the social system. Use our gay and transgendered friends to help with this. This is a natural movement for our liberal faculty members at colleges and universities who despise the Enemy and long for new ideas and movements to undercut traditional values and concepts. They can also make more money writing articles, books, and giving speeches on the subject that they claim only they really know about.

Colleges can now add some courses and even majors that will help students learn all about numerous genders and what some of their options might be in deciding what gender they really are.

Think of all the new pronouns that will be needed and all the new words that can be added to the dictionary. Also glory in the confusion this will sew in young students and their inter-gender relationships. The confusion and damage that this will bring about will seriously undermine the Enemy's horrid plan for solid male/female families raising strong generations of young people who oppose Father Satan. All the things I have mentioned here must be pursued as fast as possible. You can brush aside the Enemy's followers and their argument by labeling them as religious fanatics putting forward outdated ideas. Full speed ahead!

Your Magnificent and Humble Professor,

X

Luscious Academianut Ph.D.

P.S. We're thrilled by the uni-sex bathrooms and the fact that men can say they are a woman on any particular day and use a bathroom with them. Encourage more corporations like the Target company that are creating bathrooms for all sexes and doing all they can to do away with sexual differences in presenting their products including eliminating pink and blue colors on toys. Punish the American Family Association (AFA) for their boycott of Target because of Target's new policies.

LETTERS FROM PERVERSE UNIVERSITY

Following is one of a series of letters intercepted by Dr. L. James Harvey. They are from a Professor of Deception at Perverse University in Hell and are sent to his former students who are in the U.S.A. working to tempt America away from its Judeo/Christian values. Dr. Harvey has edited the profanity out of the letters and presents them for your information.

Perverse University ™

Department of Deception
P.O. Box 666
Smoke City, Hades 66666

Home of the Fighting Red Devils

Paul Harvey Revisited

Dear Reader,

Instead of a new letter from P.U. I decided to share with you a prediction and prophesy outlined by Paul Harvey (1919-2009), one of the greatest radio broadcasters of all time. In 1965 Harvey outlined how he, if he was our Father Satan, would take down America. I'm sending it because it is exactly what we must continue to do. Harvey was right and we've made progress on the plan he outlined, but there's more to do. Harvey outlines what was going to happen if the U.S. in the 1960s continued on its path of throwing away its Judeo/Christian values for those of the secular humanists. He was right! Here is what Paul Harvey (no relation, by the way) said in 1965.

"If I were the devil....if I were the prince of darkness, I'd want to engulf the whole world in darkness, and I'd have a third of its real estate and four fifths of its population, but I wouldn't be happy until I seized the ripest apple on the tree – (read the U.S.A.).

So, I'd set about however necessary to take over the United States. I'd subvert the churches first -- I'd begin with a campaign of whispers. With the wisdom of a serpent, I would whisper to you as I whispered to Eve, "Do as you please." To the young I would whisper, "The Bible is a myth."

I would convince them that man created God instead of the other way around. I would confide that what is bad is good, and what is good is "square." And the old, I would teach to pray after me, "Our Father which art in Washington."

And then I'd get organized. I'd educate authors on how to make the lurid exciting, so that anything else would appear dull and uninteresting. I'd threaten TV with dirtier movies and vice versa. I'd infiltrate unions and urge more loafing and less work, because idle hands usually work for me. I'd pedal narcotics to whom I could. I'd sell alcohol to ladies and gentlemen of distinction. I'd tranquilize the rest with pills.

If I were the devil, I'd soon have families at war with themselves, churches at war with themselves, and nations at war with themselves; until each in its turn was consumed, and with promises of higher ratings, I'd have mesmerizing media fanning the flames.

If I were the devil, I would encourage schools to refine young intellectuals, and neglect to discipline emotions – just let those run wild, until before you know it, you'd have to have drug sniffing dogs and metal detectors at every schoolhouse door.

Within a decade, I'd have the prisons overflowing. I'd have judges promoting pornography – soon I could evict God from the courthouse, and then the schoolhouse, and then from the house of Congress. And in his own churches I would substitute psychology for religion and deify science. I would lure priests and pastors into misusing boys and girls, and church money.

If I were the devil, I would make the symbol for Easter an egg and the symbol for Christmas a bottle.

If I were the devil, I would take from those who have and give it to those who wanted until I had killed the incentive of the ambitious. What do you bet I could get whole states to promote gambling as the way to get rich? I would question against extremes and hard work, and patriotism, and moral conduct. I would convince the young that marriage is old fashioned, that swinging is more fun, that what you see on TV is the way to be. And thus,

I could undress you in public, and I could lure you into bed with diseases for which there is no cure.

In other words, if I were the devil, I'd just keep on doing what he's doing.

Paul Harvey, good day.

Following is one of a series of letters intercepted by Dr. L. James Harvey. They are from a Professor of Deception at Perverse University in Hell and are sent to his former students who are in the U.S.A. working to tempt America away from its Judeo/Christian values. Dr. Harvey has edited the profanity out of the letters and presents them for your information.

Perverse University ™

Department of Deception
P.O. Box 666
Smoke City, Hades 66666

Home of the Fighting Red Devils

Evolution Emergency

Dear Truthtwister,

We have a serious emergency and I've never seen our Father Satan so upset. He finally heard that our essential theory of evolution is under serious attack and may fall as the anti-god explanation for the existence of life on earth. You were so successful in getting Charles Darwin, 160 years ago, to help us develop a godless theory for life that excluded the Enemy, and which allowed us to throw creation and the Enemy out of all public education in the U.S. That gave our atheistic and secular humanist educators full reign to make a god out of man and to teach our values. As late as 2009, 87% of all scientists agreed with evolutionary theory. Now all of this is seriously threatened and you allowed it to happen. How could you permit this?

Father Satan heard that 1000 of the most prestigious scientists worldwide have signed a document that states, "We are skeptical of claims for the ability of random mutation and natural selection to account for the complexity of life." This undermines Darwin and these scientists are from some of the most elite institutions in the world including Harvard, Yale, MIT, the University of Cambridge, Moscow State University, Ben-Gurion University, the Smithsonian, Princeton University, and other institutions in Brazil, Hong Kong, South Africa, France, and the Czech Republic. Horrible, horrible! A worldwide refutation of evolution.

At the same time, one of the scientists most responsible for the development of the Intelligent Design theory, Dr. Michael Behe, has published a new book entitled "Darwin Devolves: The New Science DNA That Challenges Evolution." He destroys Darwin with scientific evidence and with Darwin's own logic. As you know, before Darwin died, which was before cellular science had unraveled the secrets of DNA, he said if our cells contained further complex mechanisms related to life then his theory would be incorrect. Now that has happened and scientists worldwide are being convinced that the complex and wonderous hereditary architecture found in our human cells could never have been created by random accident. Scientists worldwide will now be left to seriously consider that there had to be an intelligent designer, which will ultimately lead them to the Enemy. This is a disaster. Our principal building block for godlessness has been kicked out from underneath us. Now you know why Father Satan is so mad.

You must be prepared for the worst. All those awards you received in building up evolution, and getting creation kicked out of American education, may now be withdrawn. Worst of all, you may be fired and recalled. I can't even promise you a return to your professorship here at P.U. Those must be approved by Father Satan and he's in no mood to do so. He may calm down but don't count on this. The demise of evolution opens the door for the Enemy's scientists to make major advances in proving that the Enemy is the creator of all things – a belief we must fight with everything we have. Develop a plan of attack. It might save your life.

Your Brilliant and Positively Devious Professor,

X

Luscious Academianut Ph.D.

Following is one of a series of letters intercepted by Dr. L. James Harvey. They are from a Professor of Deception at Perverse University in Hell and are sent to his former students who are in the U.S.A. working to tempt America away from its Judeo/Christian values. Dr. Harvey has edited the profanity out of the letters and presents them for your information.

Perverse University ™

Department of Deception
P.O. Box 666
Smoke City, Hades 66666

Home of the Fighting Red Devils

Lowering Higher Education

Dear Eddown,

Father Satan was praising you the other day for the great work you have done in taking the public education system in the USA down. He praised you for getting prayer, Bible reading, and the 10 Commandments thrown out of the public schools of America. Then you got them to teach evolution as a scientific fact and essentially establish our religion of secular humanism as the only acceptable one. Best of all you got the American educational system to reinterpret the First Amendment to the Constitution to mean it is not freedom of religion in America, but freedom from religion that is the right. Based on this reinterpretation, everything Christian continues to be thrown out. And now you have the LGBTQ community working hard and successfully to defeat Christianity because most Christians oppose sodomy. With their help throughout the schools of America we can produce generation after generation of atheists to help take the US down. So, you get a heap of praise for undermining the Judeo/Christian value base upon which America was founded. It insures our ultimate victory.

Father Satan had some good words for your work in higher education also. He was particularly happy about the way you have taken a basic educational value and twisted it to our cause. He was referring to the concept of diversity.

It used to mean that good education welcomed a variety of ideas which leads to honest and full debate thereby helping students think through complex issues to arrive at reasoned and logical conclusions. So, diversity of ideas was essential to good education. Now you have twisted this basic idea to mean diversity and inclusion and you have wedded it to the social justice movement, focused it on racial, sexual, and political matters, and now cause the movement to take on such a strong liberal political element, which includes our LGBTQ friends, that on many campuses the diversity and inclusion groups try to silence anyone who disagrees with them. They actually produce colleges and universities which prohibit or severely limit freedom of speech and the sharing of diverse opinions. They refuse to let Christians present their faith and do not allow speakers with diverse positions to theirs on campus. They have twisted a basic educational value to serve their own (and our) values. They label anyone or group committed to the Enemy and his horrid book as bigots, homophobes, racists, and sexists. Wonderful! And all in the name of education. Hypocrisy has always served us well, as long as it stays hidden.

We are thrilled to learn that the student loan debt has now reached 1.5 trillion dollars. The profligate spending in higher ed has been passed on to students who have had to borrow to stay in college. This debt is keeping a whole generation from starting their lives as others have by getting married, buying a house, and starting a family. And what has all that money bought? This is what pleases us – more administrators, new buildings, and new programs that do not lead to jobs. For the first time in history colleges have more administrators than faculty members. What faculty colleges do have are overwhelmingly liberal and secular and they are not teaching they are indoctrinating. Our values are being passed on and the Enemy's values are being driven off campus. We're winning all the way around and helping damage a whole generation of American students in the process. Keep up the great work.

Father Satan wants you to work harder to take down those colleges still committed to the Enemy. They are working to control costs and they still produce soldiers for the Enemy. Make sure our popular secular values seep into the DNA of these colleges and undermine the values of the Enemy.

Remember, if you can get an institution dedicated to the Enemy to begin to compromise their values, you can turn them into one of those wonderful lukewarm Christian institutions. The Enemy hates lukewarmness and cowardess among his people because it serves our cause better than his. Encourage more of it!

It will be a long hard fight but we're winning so keep up the good work and do everything you can to lower higher education in America.

Your Exquisitely Brilliant Professor,

X

Luscious Academianut Ph.D.

LETTERS FROM PERVERSE UNIVERSITY

Following is one of a series of letters intercepted by Dr. L. James Harvey. They are from a Professor of Deception at Perverse University in Hell and are sent to his former students who are in the U.S.A. working to tempt America away from its Judeo/Christian values. Dr. Harvey has edited the profanity out of the letters and presents them for your information.

Perverse University ™

Department of Deception
P.O. Box 666
Smoke City, Hades 66666

Home of the Fighting Red Devils

Abortion Demise

Dear Child Killer,

Father Satan is deeply concerned that the U.S. may be moving toward over turning the Roe v Wade decision and undermining the right to abort unborn children. We can't let this hard-won decision be lost. Since that wonderful court victory in 1973 over 60 million unborn children have been killed in the U.S. That's simply marvelous. However, we can't relax, the Enemy and his forces are attacking with vengeance. As I wrote you earlier, you must kill the confirmation of Supreme Court Justice Brett Kavanaugh. In spite of what he says about Roe being "settled law," he could still vote to overturn a case he believed was wrongly decided. He could still determine that there is no right in the Constitution for abortion. We can't take the chance on him.

We are also upset down here that the information about the Roe v Wade case is becoming known publicly. You must cover up that "Jane Doe" in that case was actually Norm McCorvey and that she was not raped, as stated in the case, but became pregnant consensually with a boy-friend. It also hurts our case when she tells how she was recruited by our lawyers and mistreated by them so they could bring a case against anti-abortion laws. Our cause has been hurt by having McCorvey actually become a servant of the Enemy and an anti-abortion activist working against us, Fortunately, she now has died but her story lingers and must be destroyed through a campaign of lies, which counter her horrid assertions.

You must also work to make sure the various States don't continue to limit abortions and that the U.S. Congress does not take up the "Unborn Child Protection Act" (UCPA) again. Thank Satan that our Democrat friends in the Senate kept the Republicans from winning a cloture vote on that act 51 to 46. That's too close after the House passed it 237 to 187. If the Republicans get to 60 votes or if the Senate changes its rules to allow it to pass by a simple majority our goose is cooked. We need for our Democrats to win the House in November to protect our gains. The UCPA which prohibits abortions after the unborn child can feel pain at the 20-week development point would seriously hurt our cause. You just can't let that ever pass. Do whatever you can undermine Senator Lindsey Graham who has been promoting the UCPA and is committed to ensuring that it passes.

You must also do everything you possibly can to defend Planned Parenthood. Make sure these efforts to defund them nationally and in several states fail. As you well know, Planned Parenthood is the leading proponent and provider of abortions. We were disturbed down here that the California Law forcing Christian health centers to advertise abortion as a health alternative failed. See if it can be slightly reworded and passed again in the California legislature. Our Democrat friends in California and that wonderful 9th Circuit Court have been good to us. Use them all you can!

Your Magnificent Professor,

X

Luscious Academianut Ph.D.

LETTERS FROM PERVERSE UNIVERSITY

Following is one of a series of letters intercepted by Dr. L. James Harvey. They are from a Professor of Deception at Perverse University in Hell and are sent to his former students who are in the U.S.A. working to tempt America away from its Judeo/Christian values. Dr. Harvey has edited the profanity out of the letters and presents them for your information.

Perverse University ™

Department of Deception
P.O. Box 666
Smoke City, Hades 66666

Home of the Fighting Red Devils

Our Democrat Success

Dear Nationdown,

As you remember, Father Satan's long-term plan to destroy America included trying to get one of the American political parties to join our ranks to pass legislation to destroy the laws that had been passed based on the Judeo/Christian beliefs of the founders. We now believe, because of your good work, that we have captured the Democrat Party. We are certain they will now continue our efforts to take America down.

We were thrilled when the Democrats lustily booed the reinstatement of the words God and Jerusalem in the Democrat Platform at their 2012 national Convention after their platform committee had purposefully removed them. While we partied down here over that event, we still weren't sure we had captured the party, however, recent events indicate that the victory is ours.

We rejoiced recently when the Democrat New York State Senate passed, and the then Catholic governor of New York signed into law, an abortion bill that permits late term, even after a live birth from a botched abortion, killing of babies. Fantastic! And this further weakened the Catholic Church when they did nothing to Governor Andrew Cuomo, a Catholic. Virginia and other states are considering similar legislation all supported by our

Democrat friends who have surrendered to the women's rights activists on the matter. We also had the Santa Barbara Community College Board in California, who are Democrats, decide to eliminate the Pledge of Allegiance from their board meetings because it includes the "under God" phrase. Marvelous! Let this begin a wonderful movement nationwide. We also heard a group of Democrats in the House of Representatives want to remove "so help me God" from the swearing in oath witnesses take before their Natural Resources Committee. Yes! We've waited so long for America to deny and destroy its religious heritage and now we have the results of our good work supported whole heartedly by the Democrat party.

We are also encouraged by the statements of two new elected Democrat Representatives who are Moslems and have indicated they are following the Koran in its clear opposition to Jews and Christians. Rashida Talib of Michigan and Ilham Omar of Minnesota both elected from large populations of Moslems in those states, who have largely not assimilated into American society. We need more of this from balkanized racial and ethnic groups who prefer their own religion to the Judeo/Christian ones. Work hard on the Asian and Indian enclaves in the U.S. to elect Buddhists and Hindus to national offices where they can also vote to undermine these foundational American values.

Continue to increase the pressure our LGBTQ friends are putting on Christian businesses nationwide to deny their Christian beliefs and perform functions that reinforce homosexual values they don't believe in, and which that horrid book of the Enemy says are sinful. Keep the pressure on! Defeat those horrid Christian legal groups that are defending those, Christians.

We are also excited by the anti-white toxic masculine racism which our Democrat friends have put forth, and which holds such marvelous potential for us. Use the fact that white males were largely responsible for the founding values imbedded in major American national and state constitutions and documents. Push the toxic white masculine theme, particularly if we can find some slave owners among them. We can then take them and America down. We can see our Democrat friends forcing schools, states, cities and others to remove George Washington's name from schools, streets etc. because he was a toxic white male slave owner. I don't know why we didn't go down this path sooner. It looks like a winner. Jefferson, Madison and others should be on the list. Our wonderful liberal college and university professors and Democrat activists need to push this movement with everything they've got. See to it! And keep up the great work. We've got America on the downward slide, push them harder.

Your brilliant and Insightful Professor,

X

Luscious Academianut Ph.D.

P.S. See if you can get some Democrats in the House of Representatives to introduce a bill to take "In God we Trust" off all American money. If you can't do that, have them add an "ed" to the word trust <G>. Just an example of my superior sense of humor.

P.S. 2 Use the fact that Senator Chuck Schumer, the majority leader in the Senate, and Nancy Pelosi, the Speaker in the House of Representatives, both Roman Catholics, support abortion on demand and the implementation of gay rights, both positions which are contrary to the teachings of the Pope and Catholic Church. Use this information to weaken the faith of the Christians left in the church.

Following is one of a series of letters intercepted by Dr. L. James Harvey. They are from a Professor of Deception at Perverse University in Hell and are sent to his former students who are in the U.S.A. working to tempt America away from its Judeo/Christian values. Dr. Harvey has edited the profanity out of the letters and presents them for your information.

Perverse University ™

Department of Deception
P.O. Box 666
Smoke City, Hades 66666

Home of the Fighting Red Devils

Support Soros

Dear Destabilizer,

I'm writing to ask you to do everything possible to keep George Soros alive and to promote everything he's doing to help us destroy the U.S.A. As you'll remember, Soros was born in Hungary in 1930 as Gyorgy Schwartz of non-observant Jewish parents, changed his name to George Soros, became a billionaire, and became an American citizen. His work to destroy the Judeo/Christian culture in the U.S. is particularly pleasing to Father Satan since it's one of the Enemy's chosen people (a Jew), who is doing everything he can to take Christian America down. You must help him. Do everything you can to help his Open Society Foundation, to whom Soros has given $32 Billion dollars, to fund programs that will undermine and destroy American society and the Judeo/Christian values upon which it was founded.

Soros, now an American citizen, is so bad he is un welcome in the country of his birth, because he and his organizations have been working to undermine the democratic Hungarian government one of the U.S.A.s closest allies in Europe.

By the way, Soros' money is at work in over 100 countries in the world as he works diligently to force countries into a global one world government with a one global currency, which he will control, and on which he will get even richer. Some of our soldiers have been very successful in Europe particularly in England, France, and Italy using Soros's organizations and people to sow discord. You should check with headquarters in those countries to find out what has worked best for them.

In the meantime, keep doing what is working so well for you. Helping Soros by electing prosecutors in large Democrat cities where they can fail to prosecute looters, rioters, drug offenders and protect their sanctuary city status. This is having wonderful effects on crime rates and public confidence with their shrinking police departments. Soros's money has already elected prosecutors in several large cities including Los Angeles, St. Louis, Portland, Seattle, and Chicago. These prosecutors are releasing drug offenders, are failing to prosecute property crimes like auto theft and shoplifting, and are anti-police. Some of these cities are becoming unlivable because of the crime increase and the failure to protect the citizens. This creates the kind of chaos we like and in which we can create the kind of uprisings that could foster civil disobedience and even bring state and local governments down.

One caution, however, if things get too bad, particularly with the lock downs caused by the virus, there could be successful recall elections, which will sideline some of our best compatriots. Do what you can to kill the recall efforts in California, Michigan, and New York City. We can't afford to lose our friends there.

Also, since Soros is getting up there in age, work to help identify and train a successor so that when Soros comes to join us down here there will be someone to continue his good work.

Your Most Competent and Glorious Professor,

X

Luscious Academianut Ph.D.

Following is one of a series of letters intercepted by Dr. L. James Harvey. They are from a Professor of Deception at Perverse University in Hell and are sent to his former students who are in the U.S.A. working to tempt America away from its Judeo/Christian values. Dr. Harvey has edited the profanity out of the letters and presents them for your information.

Perverse University ™

Department of Deception
P.O. Box 666
Smoke City, Hades 66666

Home of the Fighting Red Devils

The Prager List

Dear Faithdown,

As you know, Dennis Prager is one of our most hated people in the U.S. He's a Jew and one of the worst writers and radio/tv talk show hosts when it comes to exposing our activities to take down the USA. He recently wrote an article exposing the lies we want the young people of America to believe. While the article exposes us, it also gives some clarity to our soldiers in the U.S. working with young people. Because it so clearly uncovers what we are trying to do I'm sending you a list of the lies so you can circulate it to your soldiers to help clarify their focus on what we need to teach the young people of America. The clarity with which Prager does this should remind you and you compatriots how dangerous this Prager is. Undermine him whenever you have the chance. Here is the list of lies he developed: (This list appeared in the Whistleblower magazine Jan. 2020 and is slightly altered and abbreviated here.)

1. If you are a young black, you need to know the country loathes you. You are more likely to be expelled from school, shot by the police, disproportionately imprisoned, and discriminated against than whites your whole life.

2. If you're a young girl know that you will be paid less than males for the same work, are likely to be sexually molested, and there is a "glass ceiling" that will prevent your professional success. You should also believe that professional success is far more important than marriage and family to your future.

3. If you are a young Latino know the white majority is so xenophobic that it would, if it could, expel you from the country. You are unwelcomed here.

4. If you are a white male, you are the recipient of unearned privilege, and you're a racist.

5. Boys and girls should know there is actually no such thing as "boys and girls" and your teachers are told to refer to you only as "students" not 'boys and girls."

6. Young people should know there is no God. So, don't look to God or religion for meaning. Religion is for the emotionally handicapped. Look for meaning in social action.

7. The Christian religion, the faith of most of Americans since its founding, approved of slavery, the slaughter of native Americans, and the persecution of gays. Most people who call themselves Christian's today are bigots and hypocrites. Whatever good has been done in America has been done by enlightened secularists. Islam is the religion of peace.

8. Western civilization is not morally superior to any other and in many ways it's worse. It has been responsible for persecutions and genocide. That's why we celebrate Indigenous People's Day not Columbus Day.

9. Most American holidays are meaningless (except for Halloween) and should not be celebrated. President's birthdays like Washington and Lincoln should be forgotten. Many were rich white slaveholders. July 4 wasn't the founding of the U.S. 1619 was when the first slaves reached America in Virginia. Memorial Day is just another day off, most of

the deceased died in vain anyway. Use the typical holidays for personal pleasure.

10. You have few American heroes. Most currently celebrated heroes were rich white men who believed in patriarchy, slavery and the suppression of women. They were all racists and some were rapists. In short, you have few, if any, heroes.

We've got to get these messages to the young people of America. Use the liberal teachers we have worked so hard to get into the schools of America and ensure that the liberal professors in the colleges and universities keep producing teachers for the schools who will keep these values coming.

Your Brilliant and Inciteful Professor,
X
Luscious Academianut Ph.D.

LETTERS FROM PERVERSE UNIVERSITY

Following is one of a series of letters intercepted by Dr. L. James Harvey. They are from a Professor of Deception at Perverse University in Hell and are sent to his former students who are in the U.S.A. working to tempt America away from its Judeo/Christian values. Dr. Harvey has edited the profanity out of the letters and presents them for your information.

Perverse University ™

Department of Deception
P.O. Box 666
Smoke City, Hades 66666

Home of the Fighting Red Devils

Bureaucratic Bliss

Dear Nationkiller,

As I mentioned last month, I wanted to write to emphasize how critical it is for you to continue to do everything you can to facilitate the growth of the American governmental bureaucracy. As in all failed societies in the past, governments grew until they absorbed all of the resources their societies needed to grow and prosper.

That great 20th century management consultant, Peter Drucker pointed to our ultimate goals when he said two critical things about bureaucracies. First, he said that bureaucracies are organizations in which the employees have come to misconceive themselves as ends and the organization as a means, and second, he said that most bureaucracies will grow at the rate of 4.7% a year regardless of the work that needs to be done. Do you see the beauty in that? It means as bureaucracies grow, they lose sight of why they were created, become self-absorbed, and focus entirely on their own growth and preservation. There are internal factors that pressure the government to spend more, add more programs, grow the staff, and above all, particularly if they are unionized, resist any attempts to review, revise, or cut programs. Bureaucracies add but they cannot subtract! Add to this the fact that bureaucracies average 10% waste, fraud, and abuse every year and we have the picture of a cancer on society that can be fatal.

We already have America in the latter stages of bureaucratic failure. The U.S. government cannot cut its spending even though it is $30 trillion in debt and projecting it to be $40 trillion in the next decade. Congress is so corrupt and beholden to outside financial interests with tax breaks, special programs, and favors that they can't cut anything of significance. Government employees already make twice the wages of private sector workers doing similar work and incompetent federal employees can't be fired because of union protection. Do you see the beauty and potential in all this for us? America will continue to grow the bureaucratic beast, run up the debt, pay for it by printing fiat money, debase the dollar, and surrender America's world leadership. We have the U.S. on the same path that destroyed 27 complex societies before it over the last 4500 years, as I wrote you in last month's letter. Make sure the wealthy and the bureaucracy suck all the productive resources out of the American society.

We must pressure the government to raise taxes and grow bigger until they drain all the productive resources out of the economy leaving a debt that is un-payable and the U.S. in a wonderful state of bankruptcy. The Enemy said it best in his horrible book, "The borrower is a slave to the lender." The U.S. is fast becoming the slave. Keep up the great work. Make sure the Federal Reserve continues its printing of money. No tapering. They've already printed trillions of fiat dollars in their attempts to save the rich bankers and wealthy. Make them continue to believe they can print their way out of debt. Be sure they don't confront the truth that every civilization in the past that has tried this failed miserably.

Be careful, however, you've got to make sure those horrid conservatives go away. Many of the Enemy's people are being attracted to their smaller government, balanced budget, pay down the debt, and lower taxes message. Get the secular media to paint all conservatives as people who are uneducated bigots, homophobes, and religious zealots. Neutralize them! Keep up the good work! They're on the run.

Your Magnificent and Gifted Professor,

X

Luscious Academianut Ph.D.

LETTERS FROM PERVERSE UNIVERSITY

Following is one of a series of letters intercepted by Dr. L. James Harvey. They are from a Professor of Deception at Perverse University in Hell and are sent to his former students who are in the U.S.A. working to tempt America away from its Judeo/Christian values. Dr. Harvey has edited the profanity out of the letters and presents them for your information.

Perverse University ™

Department of Deception
P.O. Box 666
Smoke City, Hades 66666

Home of the Fighting Red Devils

Euphemism Sunday

Dear Distortion,

I'm writing to inform you that our Father Satan has finally agreed to set aside one day a year to celebrate the euphemisms you and your colleagues have used to advance our cause in the U.S. Your former professors Dr. Oral Rubbish and Dr. Verbal Smut were particularly influential in persuading our Father Satan that these language distortions have been instrumental in our success in the U.S. So now once a year on the third Sunday in March your marvelous work in using euphemisms will be celebrated all over Hell.

We think it was your fine work in the gay marriage area in the U.S. that finally convinced our Father that language can and has played a critical part in our work in the U.S.A., and we did it with the aid of the intellectually elite and Christian liberals, which makes our success even sweeter. Instead of talking about sodomy, that sexual sin the Enemy hates so much, Americans talked about gay love and rights. Never once, that we could find, did a major American media figure ever mention sodomy when discussing gay marriage. It was always framed as an issue of love and rights, concepts to which Americans automatically genuflect. Divorcing sodomy, which has for over 5000 years been considered a perverse sexual practice and a sin, from gay marriage and instead dressing it up in love and rights was sheer genius and insured a victory for us before we even began to fight. Fantastic!

When some perverse Christians tried to raise the issue of sodomy, HIV/Aids, and sexually transmitted diseases, you properly slammed the door on them by labeling them bigots and homophobes. We applaud you for the way you handled that opposition, it was pure genius the way you made evil sound good by re-labeling it.

We've also celebrated the other euphemisms you've so effectively used. Dressing up the killing of unborn children as women's health and rights was great too. Using free speech to cover up pornography, lotteries as promoting education, gambling as promoting the welfare of native Americans, pedophilia as simply man/boy love, permissive child rearing as building self-esteem, evolution as scientific fact, materialism as a sign of the Enemy's blessings, marijuana as a medical necessity, the use of hard drugs as mind expansions, and the Bible as an outdated book of fairy tales are just some of the marvelous linguistic tools you have used to cover up the sins and falsehoods we have worked so hard to promote in the U.S. They have played a major role in allowing Americans to accept and practice sinful behavior while rationalizing it with one or more of your beautiful verbal evasions from the truth. You are a genius.

I must keep reminding you, however, that even with our great successes in the U.S.A. there is a strong latent army of the Enemy's people who could rise up and threaten our progress toward immorality. You must do everything you can to stifle their prayer lives and their attempts to unify their forces and counter attack. Demean and diminish the influence of any evangelical leader that steps forward and kill that horrible conservative MAGA movement in the Republican Party. Keep up the good work. We're winning! Don't let up!

You Magnificent and Humble Professor,

X

Luscious Academianut Ph.D.

🗲 LETTERS FROM PERVERSE UNIVERSITY 🗲

Following is one of a series of letters intercepted by Dr. L. James Harvey. They are from a Professor of Deception at Perverse University in Hell and are sent to his former students who are in the U.S.A. working to tempt America away from its Judeo/Christian values. Dr. Harvey has edited the profanity out of the letters and presents them for your information.

Perverse University ™

Department of Deception
P.O. Box 666
Smoke City, Hades 66666

Home of the Fighting Red Devils

Pornography

Dear Pornup,

I can't tell you how proud we are of your success in submerging the American culture in pornography. Once the Supreme Court lowered the bars on pornography and labeled it acceptable free speech you ran with the ball in exemplary fashion. As we planned down here earlier, we knew that pornography would undermine the American family and lead to some delicious results for us. You're now reaping the benefits of open sexual conduct in broken families, children born out of wedlock, and a level of immorality that is magnificent, as it breaks down the American character. We're winning big in large part due to your work. A recent study we just saw indicated that 68% of Christian men and 50% of their pastors visit pornographic sites regularly. Marvelous! We just heard another popular Christian theologian has fallen to adultery, and the grandson of Billy Graham too, – wonderful! When Christian men sin, we win. Women are increasingly being drawn to the porno sites as well, which divorce sex from love and make it a self-indulgent pleasure centered sin. We win when this happens. And just recently we had that wonderful web site Ashley Madison exposed for promoting adultery among married couples. Fantastic! America is going down the slippery slope faster than we hoped.

The internet has obviously been a big help in spreading pornography. 90% of youth ages 12-18 now use the internet regularly. We need to make it their most important sexual educator. Children can easily avoid parental controls and view even the most hardcore sexual material. Recent research shows the average age of first exposure to pornography is 9 years of age. Children exposed to porn engage in sexual acts at earlier ages, have more STDs, unwanted pregnancies, and negative psychological and emotional consequences. No wonder there are so many cases of teachers having sex with students even in middle schools. Stimulate them and they will fall. The hooking up culture in colleges and universities is another great result of pornography and the decline of morality in the U.S.

As we taught you here at P.U., if we can destroy the Enemy's plan for marriage between a man and a woman raising children in a loving environment, we can undermine the moral fabric of the U.S. 41% of children in the U.S. are now born out of wedlock (that's' over 70% among blacks) and 50% will never live with both natural parents. Little chance the children will develop the kind of moral character that made America great in the past. Even Franklin Graham recently decried the moral decline in the U.S. and admitted we are winning the battle there. Great! Keep the pressure on.

You must continue to blunt all attempts to restrict pornographic material. Stop organizations like Enough is Enough (EIE) from passing legislation to protect children from porn. Continue to ride that horse that pornography is harmless and actually beneficial to healthy sexual relations between caring adults. That lie has served us well ride it for all you can.

Continue to use the LGBT crowd to help destroy marriages. The research from European countries, which have had gay marriage for many years, indicates that gay marriage tends to undermine all marriages, contrary to what they claim. Where they've had gay marriage for years fewer people bother to marry and the divorce rate goes up. The gays are on our side. Encourage their attacks on Christian businesses that won't serve them and take away all tax exemptions from Christian organizations, churches, and colleges that teach that sodomy is a sin and oppose gay marriages. Support those efforts any way you can. Destruction of the American family and the Christian church lie at the heart of our strategy – never forget that and we'll win big.

Your Increasingly Brilliant Professor,

X

Luscious Academianut Ph.D.

Following is one of a series of letters intercepted by Dr. L. James Harvey. They are from a Professor of Deception at Perverse University in Hell and are sent to his former students who are in the U.S.A. working to tempt America away from its Judeo/Christian values. Dr. Harvey has edited the profanity out of the letters and presents them for your information.

Perverse University ™

Department of Deception
P.O. Box 666
Smoke City, Hades 66666

Home of the Fighting Red Devils

Push Muslim Immigration!

Dear Nationdown,

The Trump administration stopped our good work in getting Muslims to immigrate in large numbers to undermine the Christian foundation of the U.S. Trump used the term radical Islamic terrorists, and he reduced the number of Muslim refugees, which hurt our cause. Obama never mention Islam and terrorism together, and he welcomed all Muslim refugees, which helped us a great deal. Now Biden has opened the flood gates, thank Satan!

Here's something about which I must warn you, never let the Americans read the Koran. If they do, they'll find out that all Muslims are told they are to hate all Christians, Jews, and infidels. You must also keep Americans from reading the following passages in the Koran:

1. "Believers, take neither Jews or Christians for your friends." (Sura 5:51)
2. "Infidels are those who declare: 'God is the Christ' the son of Mary. (Sura 5:17)
3. "Make war on the infidels who dwell around you." (Sura 9:123)
4. "The infidels are your sworn enemies." (Sura 4:101)
5. "When you meet the infidel in battle, strike off their heads." (Sura 47:4)

6. "Mohammed is Allah's apostle. Those who follow him are ruthless to the infidels." (Sura 48:29)
7. "Kill the disbelievers wherever we find them." (Sura 2:191)

Hide from the infidels that the Koran allows Muslims to lie when making treaties and agreements, when doing so will help their cause. They are then free to break such agreements when it furthers the cause of Allah. This means that Muslims are free to act friendly and moderate until they are a majority in an area, and then they are free to treat Christians and non-Muslims as infidels.

Also hide from Americans that Islamic law enforces dhimmi status on all non-Muslims meaning they have to pay a specific tax, cannot propagate their faith, or say anything insulting about Islam. Dhimmis become second class citizens whenever Moslems are in a majority in an area.

Our danger in America is that some moderate Moslems may reject parts of the Koran and support the Americans against our Jihadi brothers. Get our radicals to threaten them and force the moderates to follow the Koran out of fear for their lives. We must undermine any move of any group of Muslims to join the moderates.

We can undermine the U.S. by open immigration of Muslims and the imposition of Sharia Law, which directly contradicts the U.S. Constitution. Emulate the great strides some of your fellow graduates of P.U. are using in England, Sweden, Denmark, Holland, Germany and France. They have "no go zones" where Sharia law is practiced and Muslims rule supreme. Use the emotions of liberal Christians to promote the increase in Muslim refugees. Blind Americans to the dangers of accepting more Muslim refugees who refuse to integrate! Blind them to what the Koran teaches. Use Islam to destroy the Enemy!

Your Masterful Professor,

X

Luscious Academianut Ph.D.

P. S. #1 Congratulations on getting the first Muslim Congressman in the U.S., Rep. Keith Ellison from Minnesota, to refuse to take his oath on a Bible, but insisted on doing it on a Koran. Allahu Akbar!! That's real progress!

P. S. #2 Father Satan reminded us at a recent seminar that atheism and the ACLU have helped us drive the Enemy out of the public schools and public facilities in the U.S. now we must use Islam to kill off what remains of Christianity in the country.

LETTERS FROM PERVERSE UNIVERSITY

Following is one of a series of letters intercepted by Dr. L. James Harvey. They are from a Professor of Deception at Perverse University in Hell and are sent to his former students who are in the U.S.A. working to tempt America away from its Judeo/Christian values. Dr. Harvey has edited the profanity out of the letters and presents them for your information.

Perverse University ™

Department of Deception
P.O. Box 666
Smoke City, Hades 66666

Home of the Fighting Red Devils

Obama/Trump Hypocrisy Award

Dear Truthtwister,

I'm excited to tell you we have awarded our 2021 Hypocrisy award to Presidents Obama and Trump. We did a joint award for the first time because the hypocrisy they both committed over the U.S. Budget is exceptional. Their names will both be prominently displayed on the Hypocrisy Wall of Honor in the faculty lounge here at old P.U. We couldn't be prouder of your work in getting both presidents from both political parties to display a maximum dose of hypocrisy over the critical issues of government spending and the out-of-control debt which is propelling the U.S. Toward fiscal disaster.

In making the award the committee was treated to a film clip made of Senator Barak Obama when he was a U.S. Senator. The clip shows him criticizing President George W. Bush for his deficit spending, which was increasing the national debt by billions. Obama was almost in tears when he stated Bush's spending was heaping debt upon his children and grandchildren and was **immoral.** Obama stated it was impossible for him to vote for passing massive debt on future generations that had nothing to say about it. The committee was then shown a slide of the 10 trillion national debt accumulated by President Obama when he was president.

In fact, the committee broke into almost uncontrollable laughter, after it was mentioned that after calling President Bush immoral for increasing the debt, Obama piled up more debt that all the American presidents in history combined. Such hypocrisy is seldom seen by us anywhere. It's fantastic!

The committee was then presented with several clips of President Trump campaigning for office where he condemned the out-of-control spending of the Federal Government and vowed to "drain the swamp" and balance the budget. He too indicated it was immoral to pass on debt to future generations. After these clips were shown, the committee was treated to a clip of the signing of the omnibus U.S. spending bill, which was agreed by almost everyone in Washington, was one of the worst in history, and added 1.3 trillion to the Federal debt in a year or so. How fantastic and hypocritical for Trump to sign a 2500-page spending bill finished the day before, which no one had the time to read, and which was full of pork barrel spending. Put together by a few corrupt politicians, lobbyists, and congressional staffers. Trump showed exceptional hypocrisy in signing the bill when he could have vetoed it.

The beauty in all of this is the fact that the American nation was founded on the principle that no one should be taxed who did not have representation or a voice in levying the tax. This gave rise to the famous colonial war cry of "No taxation without representation." Remember the Boston Tea Party? Now America is passing debt and taxes on to future generations that have no representation and no voice in voting for the debt that is being foisted on them. Praise Father Satan for the progress we have made and for the selfish corrupt politicians who will sacrifice the countries future for their own present personal gain. We're winning big time, Marvelous! The swamp is our best weapon!

Your Perfectly Brilliant Professor,

X

Luscious Academianut Ph.D.

LETTERS FROM PERVERSE UNIVERSITY

Following is one of a series of letters intercepted by Dr. L. James Harvey. They are from a Professor of Deception at Perverse University in Hell and are sent to his former students who are in the U.S.A. working to tempt America away from its Judeo/Christian values. Dr. Harvey has edited the profanity out of the letters and presents them for your information.

Perverse University ™

Department of Deception
P.O. Box 666
Smoke City, Hades 66666

Home of the Fighting Red Devils

Antisemitism

Dear Truthless,

We have a great opportunity to wean the Democrat Party away from their commitment to their past political support of Israel and the Jews. This is a wonderful chance to increase antisemitism in the U.S. and to expand the antipathy between the political parties. You need to tie the Democrats to the Palestinians, the terrorist organization Hamas, and the world wide BDS (Boycott, Divest, Sanction) movement aimed at Israel. If you play your hand right, you might even get the Democrats to espouse Muslim causes in opposition to Jewish and Christian interests, which the Republicans tend to support.

Use these relatively new Democrat congressional representatives Ilham Omar of Minnesota and Rashida Talib of Michigan. They are both Muslims and hate Israel. They were elected from Muslim enclaves in these states. You must use the balkanization of ethnic groups, particularly Muslims, to grow and elect to political offices those who oppose the U.S. and its historic support of Israel. There are large Muslim enclaves in Southern California, in Houston, Texas, in New York City, in south Florida, in Chicago, in San Francisco, in Washington, D.C. and a few other places in the U.S. Help them grow and support Muslim and anti-Jewish causes. Get them to elect more Muslim representatives and see if you can get Omar and Talib to form an Islamic Caucus in the House of Representatives. We can then use it to oppose all Jewish and Christian issues, creating havoc in the U.S. Congress. It's worth a try! Make sure the Muslim folks hide their goal of ultimately installing Sharia Law on their way to destroying the U.S.A. and installing their world-wide Muslim Califate.

Be careful, however, not to go too far too fast, and above all else prevent anyone opposed to us from reading the Koran. Do everything you can to prevent Americans from learning about the life of the prophet Muhammed. His teachings about how to deal with infidels (Christians and Jews) can hurt us. For example, in the Koran several times Muhammed is quoted as saying infidels should be attacked: Sura 8 "…Strike off their heads then, and strike off from them every finger-tip." Sura 9…kill those who join other gods with God where ever you find them;" Sura 5 "O believers! Take not the Jews or Christians for friends." Sura 47 "When ye encounter the infidels, strike off their heads till you have made a great slaughter among them, and of the rest make fast the fetters." We love these teachings but do not let any news or TV reporters read or quote any of the above versus or other hate verses in the Koran. If they do <u>denounce them as bigots and Islamophobes.</u>

Also hide the private life of Muhammed as best you can. The fact that he had 11 wives, one married when she was only 9, while he limited his followers to 4 wives. Also hide the fact that he was a warrior leading at least 27 military campaigns and after one victory over a Jewish tribe he had all the men and boys, over 300 of them, beheaded. He took their possessions, 20% for himself and 80% split among his followers, and he took all the women and children as slaves. This was fairly common for Muhammed. Hide these facts lest they turn Americans off to a religion and leader so vicious and immoral. Make sure no Americans contrast the life of Muhammed with that of the Enemy's son. We lose big time when the two are compared.

You must also be careful not to allow any discussions of Sharia Law. Keep hidden that this is our ultimate objective. Sharia, as you know, is totally incompatible with the American Constitution. Americans must be kept in the dark about this until it is too late.

There's tremendous potential for us in this growth of Islam in the U.S. Use it to undermine the Christian foundations of American society. Look at the progress we've made in Europe. You can do this too. Full speed ahead!

Your Magnificently Brilliant Professor,

X

Luscious Academianut Ph.D.

Following is one of a series of letters intercepted by Dr. L. James Harvey. They are from a Professor of Deception at Perverse University in Hell and are sent to his former students who are in the U.S.A. working to tempt America away from its Judeo/Christian values. Dr. Harvey has edited the profanity out of the letters and presents them for your information.

Perverse University ™

Department of Deception
P.O. Box 666
Smoke City, Hades 66666

Home of the Fighting Red Devils

Destroying the Family

Dear Familydown,

Father Satan is pleased with the wonderful success you have had in destroying the American family. You have had success in undermining the Enemy's plan for building a healthy society serving him. We have received some recent data indicating that cohabitation without benefit of marriage is increasing in the U.S. Recent studies indicate that public disapproval of cohabitation is now less than 20%. While before 1960 most states had laws prohibiting cohabitation by 1998 nearly all had been repealed or ruled unconstitutional. Great work! Not only does living together without marriage defy the Enemy's guideline for raising healthy families, but new data indicates that those who cohabit are more likely to change partners, and divorce more often if they do marry, but if they have children along the way the children do less well and are more often involved in anti-social behavior than children from healthy two parent families. New research also shows that the negative effects on children from divorce and cohabitation carry over from generation to generation. That's something we have been counting on and it's happening.

The fact that Americans are waiting longer to marry gives you many years to tempt them sexually and get them to cohabit, fornicate, or become addicted to pornography. While Americans used to marry in their early 20s it's now the late 20s giving you some wonderful years to tempt them and to destroy their opportunities to have normal healthy sexual lives in a dedicated heterosexual marriage as the Enemy would desire for them.

The public schools are giving us a wonderful assist as the Enemy and the 10 Commandments have been driven out and replaced by the 10 Commandments of Liberalism, which Michael Savage in his book "Scorched Earth" lists as:

1. Man is evil and poisoning the earth.
2. The earth is a living organism and needs to be protected.
3. All white people are racists. (And toxic white males are the worst – my addition)
4. All people of color are good.
5. All refuges should be allowed in and given whatever they request.
6. If people make too much money it should be taken from them.
7. Government handouts have no price tag.
8. Nature should be protected at all costs, unless you don't like your gender.
9. Burning the American flag is protected speech.
10. All players on the international stage have equal credibility.

And these schools are producing a brainwashed, drugged, snowflake, generation of young voters who will vote for our friends in the Democrat party, if they can be persuaded to bother to vote at all, because our Democrat friends promise them the most "free stuff." We can't lose if these trends continue.

Your Magnificent, Brilliant, and humble Professor,

X

Luscious Academianut Ph.D.

Following is one of a series of letters intercepted by Dr. L. James Harvey. They are from a Professor of Deception at Perverse University in Hell and are sent to his former students who are in the U.S.A. working to tempt America away from its Judeo/Christian values. Dr. Harvey has edited the profanity out of the letters and presents them for your information.

Perverse University ™

Department of Deception
P.O. Box 666
Smoke City, Hades 66666

Home of the Fighting Red Devils

Ride Antifa

Dear Nationdown,

I couldn't wait to write you. We have a great opportunity to destroy the U.S. We can ride the George Floyd murder and the "Black Lives Matter" (BLM) movement. Hide our Antifa brothers under the BLM banner. Let Antifa be our shock troops. They've already at one point took over the center of Seattle and established a bridgehead. Their example there can serve as an example for others in some of the big cities in the U.S. Ride the movement to get rid of the police departments or make them so meek that they will refuse to oppose our well-armed Antifa shock troops. You can build on these bridgeheads and begin to unite them as we take control of the U.S. Publicize the Antifa Action Points below and use them to persuade people to join our cause. The fake news should be willing to help us. Work to get all the anti-Trump people to work with you. Encourage people to destroy all vestiges of American history including the horrible memorials in Washington D.C. like the Washington Monument, the Jefferson Memorial and the Lincoln Memorial. Take down all memorials and statutes that remind Americans of the slave holding white supremacists that founded this horrible country. In doing so you can get Americans to throw out all the remaining values of the Enemy and replace them with Father Satan's vices. We've never had a chance this good before. Don't blow it.

LETTERS FROM PERVERSE UNIVERSITY
Revolutionary Abolitionist Movement (Antifa)

10 Points of Action

1. Liberation will be won by any means necessary.
2. We will destroy the state, police, military, corporations, and all those who run the American plantation.
3. We will live in dignity in a world without prisons
4. Systems of punishment will be abolished. There will be no law to enforce, no money to protect.
5. Revolutionary justice will be determined by those who oppress.
6. There will be no government. No person or group will have power over another.
7. Communities will make decisions about how they live and will make sure everyone has what they need to live a dignified life.
8. Land is not property. It is alive, communal, and must be protected.
9. Alongside international comrades, we will destroy all borders for the free movement of people everywhere.
10. Militarist networks will defend our revolutionary communities. Liberation begins where America ends.

I can't believe how excited Father Satan is about the developments in the U.S. We were not sure we had the support we have. Our years of indoctrinating young Americans in their high schools and colleges is paying off. That and the eroding of the teachings in the Enemy's church, particularly the good work of our LGBTQ friends in undermining the truth of the Enemy's horrid book. Most of the mainline churches are lukewarm at best and will not produce any significant resistance to our movement now. There could be strong resistance from those horrible evangelicals, but I believe we now out-number them.

We have the TV on in the faculty lounge now day and night and cheer with every riot and looting we see. The development in Seattle brought cheers like I've never heard here. Keep up the great work! Take America down now before the next election. We can't run the risk that Trump's followers could win and set our cause back significantly.

Your Incredibly Gifted Professor,

X

Luscious Academianut Ph.D.

LETTERS FROM PERVERSE UNIVERSITY

Following is one of a series of letters intercepted by Dr. L. James Harvey. They are from a Professor of Deception at Perverse University in Hell and are sent to his former students who are in the U.S.A. working to tempt America away from its Judeo/Christian values. Dr. Harvey has edited the profanity out of the letters and presents them for your information.

Perverse University ™

Department of Deception
P.O. Box 666
Smoke City, Hades 66666

Home of the Fighting Red Devils

The Biden Lies

Dear Dumbdown,

Father Satan is furious that you did not kill the book, "Laptop from Hell." Now it's out and we have to deal with all the lies and misbehavior of our friends. Father Satan believes there is so much illegal and immoral behavior documented on Hunter Biden that the only thing we can do is rely on Merrick Garland, the Attorney General and Christopher Wray of the FBI, to look the other way and not prosecute. Fortunately, the Democrat Party owns them and they will protect Hunter like they did Hillary when illegal acts were obviously committed. The best we can hope for is silence on the laptop from them and the fake media. However, with Joe Biden it is different. We can't hide him, or his misconduct and lies because he's president. His popularity is plunging and if it goes much lower people will call for his impeachment. Now Father Satan listed some of the lies our friend Joe has told and he has some suggestions on how to handle them. Here are some of the lies he has told:

1. Joe claimed he was descended from a coal mining family, was the first to go to college, was trained as a racial activist in Southern black churches, was at the center of the civil rights movement in Selma and Birmingham and was arrested in South Africa while trying to visit

Nelson Mandela. These are all lies but we can brush them off by saying they aren't important and Joe must have mis-spoken because these items were so long ago.

2. Joe said he went to college on a full scholarship, was a good student, graduated with three degrees and was at the top of his class in law school. There were no full scholarships, he only graduated with one degree and he was 66th in his law school class of 85. Treat these lies like the ones in #1 above.

3. For years Joe lied about the auto accident that killed his wife and daughter. He said for years that a drunk truck driver drove into his wife's car and killed her. After his telling the story numerous times the truck drivers family threaten to sue him for libel and Joe finally apologized and admitted his wife had run a stop sign and was hit by the truck. Try to kill this story if it comes up by saying its old news, Is water over the dam, and Joe probably misunderstood what happened.

4. Joe has said he never talked to Hunter about Hunter's business dealings with foreign countries or leaders and never profited from any of them. Unfortunately, one of Hunter's business partners, Tony Bobulinski, has testified that he was in meetings where Joe talked to foreign businessmen and he testified that Joe was the "Big Guy" mentioned in emails as getting a share of the proceeds. Unfortunately, there are also bank records showing Hunter and Joe had some joint bank accounts. This is more serious and we must get everyone to deny the truth here and blame Trump supports for trying to frame Joe and Hunter. Our pals in the fake news will buy it and if repeated enough it will become truth to our supporters.

5. Joe said he never blackmailed the president of the Ukraine to fire the prosecutor who was investigating the corrupt Ukrainian company Burisma where Hunter was on the board making $83,333 a month to serve and connect them to power. Unfortunately, Joe was taped making the threat and the prosecutor was fired and the investigation went away. A Ukrainian court investigated the matter and ruled in April of 2020 in the Kyiv District Court that Joe Biden was guilty of a crime against

the prosecutor, General Viktor Shokin, for falsely getting him fired. Fortunately, we got all this covered up and it didn't hurt his election chances. Now just say that is old news, water over the dam, and was just Republicans trying to hurt Joe's chances to become president.

6. Joe said Hunter never got any money from the Chinese nor was involved in business with them. Again, it's unfortunate that there are emails and bank records that tell a different story. Hunter even today seemingly owns a 10% share in a large Chinese investment fund BHR Partners worth millions. He also once owned a share of the CEFC a large conglomerate directly tied to the Chinese Communist Party. This is also serious.

Father Satan wants all of this buried and swept under the rug. Get our friends in the fake news to dismiss all of this as old news which has been investigated and dismissed as false information put forth by Trump supporters particularly Rudy Giuliani. Make doubly sure Merrick Garland and Christopher Wray kill any attempts by staff members to open investigations on anything related to Joe or Hunter. We could lose everything we've won with Joe Biden who is well on his way to destroying the U.S.A.

Your Brilliant and Talented Professor,

X

Luscious Academianut Ph.D.

Following is one of a series of letters intercepted by Dr. L. James Harvey. They are from a Professor of Deception at Perverse University in Hell and are sent to his former students who are in the U.S.A. working to tempt America away from its Judeo/Christian values. Dr. Harvey has edited the profanity out of the letters and presents them for your information.

Perverse University ™

Department of Deception
P.O. Box 666
Smoke City, Hades 66666

Home of the Fighting Red Devils

Flag Desecration

Dear Nationdown,

We are rejoicing here at old P.U. with the success you are having in making the flag of the U.S. a symbol of hate. Americans burning and desecrating "Old Glory" and failing to stand for the singing of the Star-Spangled Banner — how good can it get for us? Using that washed up black quarterback of the San Francisco 49ers was a stroke of genius. Now you've even got 8-year-old blacks, who don't even know what's happening, turning their backs on the flag in disrespect. The best part is they are allowing whites to believe blacks are unpatriotic and are supporting the destruction of American values and traditions. Do you see how easy it is to sow dissention in people?

When Colin Kaepernick decided to kneel rather than respectfully stand for the playing of the Star-Spangled Banner, he set off a movement that is growing and expanding. You must get more black athletes in all sports to disrespect the flag. Drive a wedge between blacks and whites. Convince all blacks that the shootings of blacks by police are all racial crimes, and cover up the fact that the blacks who were shot were nearly all in the process of breaking the law. Make sure the whites are led to believe that blacks create an inordinate percentage of the crime in America and often resist arrest and incarceration. Let whites believe that blacks when they desecrate the flag are protesting American history, culture, values, and exceptionalism. This has fantastic possibilities for starting a race war and creating chaos in America. Never let the blacks realize how prosperous many blacks are or that blacks and people of color from all over the world are trying to come to America to better themselves. Also keep whites from admitting that there are a few bad cops and rare instances where they use excessive force. Keep the radical extremes on both sides from addressing the real truths here and solving the problem. Mix misunderstanding with some fanaticism on both sides to stir up the pot and lead to riots and physical confrontations.

Use the above issues, as you've begun too, to focus blacks and liberal whites on all the vestiges of slavery and the confederacy, which fought to preserve it. Have them seek to tear down all statues, flags, and symbols of the confederacy and undermine the historical validity of all Americans who either owned slaves or failed to oppose slavery all the way back to the countries founding. That would allow some to destroy the historical value of people like George Washington, Thomas Jefferson, James Madison and host of others. Do you see the beauty in this? We can undermine the history the Americans are so proud of and sow the seeds for a massive revolution that will destroy America. Propagate the big lie that American exceptionalism had nothing to do with the Enemy and his horrid values. This lie will allow America to go down that slippery slope into our secular humanism where individuals are gods and their selfish pleasures are the ultimate goal. When that ideology reigns, we win big time, as we have in countless civilizations before. Keep up the good work!

Your Handsome and Brilliant Professor,

X

Luscious Academianut Ph.D.

Following is one of a series of letters intercepted by Dr. L. James Harvey. They are from a Professor of Deception at Perverse University in Hell and are sent to his former students who are in the U.S.A. working to tempt America away from its Judeo/Christian values. Dr. Harvey has edited the profanity out of the letters and presents them for your information.

Perverse University ™

Department of Deception
P.O. Box 666
Smoke City, Hades 66666

Home of the Fighting Red Devils

Kill Freedom of Speech

Dear Prevaricator,

You need to know we drank a toast to you over the recent events at the University of California at Berkley. We can't believe how successful you were at undermining free speech and at the one university in America with which the free speech is most associated. We can't believe you pulled it off. Congratulations! We are excited now about the possibility of undermining free speech throughout higher education in America. This First Amendment principle so critical to the success of the republic is now in question. We didn't think you could undermine this principle so soon. It was a stroke of genius to have those who disagree with a point of view claim they were hurt by it and therefore it qualified as "hate speech". Disagreement equals hurt feelings, equals hate. Marvelous! Build on it! You could be in line for a major promotion, if you can keep this movement going to squelch any speech that seems offensive to our acolytes up there.

Using the LGBTQ community and the "hate speech" tool was a stroke of genius. This opens the door for any minority group who feels oppressed to oppose the speech of anyone who disagrees with them. Hate speech then becomes something everyone should oppose. It's a slight move from opposing racial or sexually oriented hate speech to opposing any speech that one considers offensive to them personally, including political speech. It was fantastic to us to see pictures of students at Berkley calling Republican's fascists because they disagreed with their political views. It gave them cover to prevent anyone from speaking who would therefore disagree with them …. and there goes free speech right out the window at the university known for free speech. Fantastic! We are almost having spontaneous orgasms we're so happy this is happening in the U.S. Free speech, one of the pillars of a free society, now threatened and on one of the most prestigious campuses in the country. Other colleges and universities are sure to follow this marvelous example.

You've got to keep our liberal friends in higher education in America from allowing any conservative or right leaning scholars and authors from speaking at their campuses. Get them to declare any speech opposing their liberal progressive agenda as "hate speech" since their speech can be labeled anti-social justice and opposed to many government programs designed to help people. Push the identification of all conservative speakers with Hitler and label them as fascists. Stir them up to the point where they believe anything, including force and rioting is acceptable to keep students from hearing their "hate speech."

Use the "Black Lives Matter" folks, the LGBTQ members, the radical feminists, and any and all left-wing groups you can find to force these speech limitations on all campuses. Have them convince the college and university administrators that they will be inviting riots, destruction of property, and excessive security costs, if these "hate speakers" are allowed on campus. Most administrators are wusses any way and they should cave in since their primary motivation is to avoid any kind of unpleasant confrontations and preserve their own jobs. Most of them are left wing liberals and will find the expression of conservative right-wing rhetoric unworthy of expression anyway.

Great work! Keep it up!

Your Brilliant and Insightful Professor,

X

Luscious Academianut Ph.D.

P.S.#1—Make sure most colleges accept the idea of establishing these "Free speech zones" on campus in out of the way places. This allows them to ban fee speech everywhere else on campus. Just what we want.

P.S.# 2—Make sure our good friend George Soros keeps funding any group that will promise to demonstrate or riot to keep conservative speakers from speaking anywhere. He has been a great help in the past.

🔱 LETTERS FROM PERVERSE UNIVERSITY 🔱

Following is one of a series of letters intercepted by Dr. L. James Harvey. They are from a Professor of Deception at Perverse University in Hell and are sent to his former students who are in the U.S.A. working to tempt America away from its Judeo/Christian values. Dr. Harvey has edited the profanity out of the letters and presents them for your information.

Perverse University ™

Department of Deception
P.O. Box 666
Smoke City, Hades 66666

Home of the Fighting Red Devils

The Unholy Alliance

Dear Confuser,

We are ecstatic about your success in bringing about the alliance of the Democrat Party and the Muslim community in America in a joint effort to take down American Christianity, capitalism, and democracy. We celebrated in the faculty lounge when we saw pictures of the so called "Squad" in the American media. These four Democrat Representatives, two avowed secularists and two committed Muslims, now represent the heart of the Democrat Party. The uniting of these two forces both dedicated to defeating the Republicans and destroying the current American capitalistic system will help ensure our success.

This alliance is not without its difficulties and you must be careful. Fortunately, the Muslims are permitted to lie about their faith and ultimate goals, as long as it furthers their ultimate objective. They can therefore present themselves to the Democrats as a loving religion only interested to the welfare of all people. Make sure they hide their commitment to implementing Sharia Law and to an international Muslim Califate. If Democrats ask about all the verses in the Koran about infidels, and the subjugation or killing of all Christians and Jews, make sure they lie and indicate that those references no longer apply and that modern Islam is all about love and peace. We are sure the Democrats will buy these lies because their joint hate of Trump, the Republicans, and modern America is so intense it will blot out all possible conflicts in uniting them in their joint aim with Islam to take down the U.S. A. and Israel as well.

The two groups are united in their support of BDS (Boycott, Divest, and Sanction) against Israel, LGBTQ rights, abortion, open borders, and they are opposed to Christianity, capitalism, and historic America including the historic founding documents ensuring freedoms including that of religion and speech. You must be sure you hide the details found in Sharia Law including their treatment of women and gays. Let the Muslims lie about these matters. Help the Muslims cover up the fact that their ultimate goal is to rule the world (their califate), and to convert everyone to Islam enslaving or killing everyone who won't convert. The joint hatred for America and former President Trump should be enough to keep them united and allow the socialist majority in the Democrat party to overlook these ultimate truths.

Work to get more Muslims elected to Congress. As the Muslim population out grows traditional Americans, and balkanizes in various parts of the U.S. they will be able to elect more like Ilhan Omar from Minnesota and Talib from Michigan, and soon could have their own Muslim caucus in Congress to harass Trump and the Republicans. Make sure all those who oppose the "Squad" members in the 2020 Congressional elections lose big time. We have a winning team here in the House of Congress don't lose this advantage.

I was also recently told the good news that the Democrat National Committee passed a resolution sponsored by the Secular Coalition of America (SCA) condemning religious liberty and welcoming to the party those who are religiously unaffiliated, namely unbelievers. The SCA represents atheists, agnostics, and humanists nationwide. This is great news for us and further drives the Enemy out of the Democrat Party. From booing the Enemy at the Democrat Party Convention in 2012 to now inviting all non-believers to the party the Democrats have stamped themselves as telling the Enemy they want no part of him or those who believe in him. The party is ours! Thank Satan.

Your Insightful and Omniscient Professor,

X

Luscious Academianut Ph.D.

P.S. we just got the wonderful news from a Wall Street Journal/NBC News study showing the values of younger generation Americans are moving in our direction. As you may have heard already, the study shows young Americans rate patriotism, religion, and having children lower than past generations. They are reflecting our values. We're winning! Keep up the good work.

Following is one of a series of letters intercepted by Dr. L. James Harvey. They are from a Professor of Deception at Perverse University in Hell and are sent to his former students who are in the U.S.A. working to tempt America away from its Judeo/Christian values. Dr. Harvey has edited the profanity out of the letters and presents them for your information.

Perverse University ™

Department of Deception
P.O. Box 666
Smoke City, Hades 66666

Home of the Fighting Red Devils

Diversity Deception

Dear Truthdown,

Father Satan was reinforcing one of his most potent weapons in defeating the Americans the other day in the faculty lounge, so, I'm passing it on to you. Father Satan indicated the most effective weapon we have is to take one of the Enemy's major instruments or truths and twist it in to a weapon for us. For example, we have turned the rainbow, which the Enemy placed in the heavens as a promise never to destroy the earth by flood again, into the flag of the gay movement. So, a positive symbol of the Enemy was turned into a symbol of sodomy, a sin which the Enemy hates. We also took the concept of love, which is the essence of the Enemy, and turned it into the reason why Americans should approve of gay marriage, and adultery of which the Enemy disapproves. Now, we want you to ride the idea of "Diversity" a concept reflecting the Enemy's creation and often thought of as a positive characteristic in education and to turn it into a vehicle for causing balkanization, distrust, and conflict in America. If diversity is a cause for unification, it hurts us, but if it produces rage and anger between groups, it is a winner for us. We can also use diversity to argue that it's a reason the LGBTQ agenda should be accepted, because in essence it's just another diverse group which strengthens America.

You must use diversity to get various groups to ruminate on injustices done to them in the past by the white power structure in America, and to demand that perceived past injustices be repaired. For example, let the blacks, browns, gays, and native Americans demand reparations for past sins by the "White" government. Increase the volume of noise by the social justice group and their screams about white supremacy. Turn diversity into a god for the liberals and democrats. Establish diversity groups on college campuses to amplify the liberal faculties claim that American History is replete with examples of injustices to minorities that need to be corrected. Make doubly sure no colleges ever create "Unity" organizations dedicated to that horrid principle of the Enemy reflecting his desire that all people amalgamate and unify in love not focus on injuries and demands for redress of grievances. Ride the critical race theory (CRT) and intersectionality movements for all they are worth to create more dissonance and division. When people frequently accuse others of misogyny, racism, homophobia, xenophobia, etc. we win and the Enemy loses. When people focus on their similarities and what unifies them, we lose. Never forget that and destroy all attempts to bring people together in the Enemy's awful concept of love. I hate to even use that word, as it is the essence of the Enemy.

Use the diversity organizations on the college campuses to drive conservative and evangelical Christian speakers away from campuses. Stress their speech is bigoted and full of hate, which should not be protected by the free speech protections of the First Amendment of the Constitution. We also need to get people to believe the U.S. Constitution is an outdated document originally put together by white males many of whom owned slaves disqualifying them from creating such a document. If we can depreciate the constitution, we can discount the First Amendment which protects free speech and the freedom of religion. This in turn will allow our followers to attack Christianity and remove all the protections and benefits (particularly their tax benefits) the U.S. gives to religions particularly those awful Christians. We're winning! Keep up the good work! Remember if we can get rid of Trump and get a wonderful liberal Democrat in the White House your work will become far easier.

Your Magnificently Brilliant Professor,

X

Luscious Academianut Ph.D.

P.S. #1—The University of California at Berkley has become an example of how we can use the diversity concept to undermine academic excellence in colleges and universities. They now worship diversity and inclusion as their highest priority. It's their god! Its now more important than academic excellence. They now spend over 20 million dollars a year on diversity and inclusion with a staff of 150 fulltime people who search the university to be sure every unit is diverse and inclusive. Highly qualified potential students and staff are disqualified while less gifted ones are selected because they meet diversity goals. See the beauty in this? We can kill the best higher education system in the world by using the diversity god. Try and get every college and university to worship diversity and inclusion over their academic excellence. It's a winner for us.

P.S. #2—There's a new book out you must undermine. That horrid writer Heather Mac Donald, the New York Times best-selling author, has published a book entitled "The Diversity Delusion." It lays bare all the great work we've done to undermine the higher education system in the U.S. We can't afford to have light shed on our work. Kill the book if you can and prevent her from any TV appearances to discuss it. Take her out if you can, she continues to hurt our cause.

⚡ LETTERS FROM PERVERSE UNIVERSITY ⚡

Following is one of a series of letters intercepted by Dr. L. James Harvey. They are from a Professor of Deception at Perverse University in Hell and are sent to his former students who are in the U.S.A. working to tempt America away from its Judeo/Christian values. Dr. Harvey has edited the profanity out of the letters and presents them for your information.

Perverse University ™

Department of Deception
P.O. Box 666
Smoke City, Hades 66666

Home of the Fighting Red Devils

Don't Kill Faith Delude It!

Dear Lukewarm,

I wanted to reinforce a truth we taught you here at P.U. in Deception 101. Remember we pointed out that the Enemy hates a weak lukewarm faith more than no faith at all. We showed you in the Enemy's horrid book in Revelations 3:17 where he said he'd spit the lukewarm out of his mouth. Your job is to get the Enemy's patients to ignore him by filling their lives with other priorities. We don't need them to deny him we just want them to disregard him. Don't even make the Enemy's patients angry with him. That reinforces their relationship and may strengthen it when the Enemy removes the cause of the anger.

No, we want the Enemy's patients to disregard him and to become lukewarm at best. This weakened form of Christianity serves as an anti-Christian vaccine, and turns off prospective patients, which is why the Enemy hates it so much.

Your job in the U.S.A. is getting easier as the society decays and so many Americans find so many of our Father Satan's distractions occupying their attention. Sex, materialism, power, hedonism, and the development of self-esteem all have the potential to drive the Enemy to a back-up position in a Christian's life. Use them! Forget non-Christians, we've got them already;

take the Enemy's patients into that lovely state of lukewarmness. Ultimately that is far better for our cause.

We recently got some data down here that indicates your efforts are paying off especially among younger Americans. We toasted you and your efforts in the faculty lounge when we got the data. According to a recent poll only 19% of all American Protestants know that salvation comes through faith, not by works, and 45% can't name the four gospels. Most fail a simple test on the essentials of their faith. Even better 81% of entering college students indicate their most important goal in life is to get rich. In 1987 85.8% said their most important goal was to develop a meaningful philosophy of life and only 41.9% saw it essential to be well off financially. What a marvelous turn around. Of the new entering students 61% favor same sex marriage, 78.4% believe abortion should be legal and 20% reported no religious affiliation at all or said they were atheistic or agnostic. Fantastic! And these are America's future leaders.

These students are, of course, the results of our getting the Enemy, prayer, and his horrid book thrown out of public education in the U.S. and having evolution taught by law. Capturing the minds of the young has always been a winning strategy for us. It's hard for a student taught they evolved from a monkey to believe in the Enemy.

One recent Christian author suggests that most Americans now have a religion he calls Moralistic Therapeutic Deism. Most may still believe in a god but they largely ignore him in their quest of for self-gratification and material success. They believe the Enemy only requires them to be nice and their future, if there is one, beyond this life is assured. See how wonderfully your efforts are paying off? We're winning!

Be sure you don't let the home school movement grow nor the private schools dedicated to the Enemy. Use the teachers' unions to help kill off these offensive institutions. Get some advice from your colleague Schooldown, who has had some good success in Sweden and Germany in killing off home schooling. Godless public schools are one of our best weapons.

Congratulations again on your great work in the U.S.A. We are on the verge of victory there.

Your Most Brilliant Professor,

X

Luscious Academianut Ph.D.

Following is one of a series of letters intercepted by Dr. L. James Harvey. They are from a Professor of Deception at Perverse University in Hell and are sent to his former students who are in the U.S.A. working to tempt America away from its Judeo/Christian values. Dr. Harvey has edited the profanity out of the letters and presents them for your information.

Perverse University ™

Department of Deception
P.O. Box 666
Smoke City, Hades 66666

Home of the Fighting Red Devils

The Language Divide

Dear Enlishdown,

I have to complement you on how well you have carried out our plan to divide the U.S. by destroying their reliance on the English language. As we taught you here at old P.U. a nation's language is a unifying factor and a common thread that holds the culture together. Undermine the common language and you cause divisions which weaken the culture. Never forget the story of how languages came about in the biblical story of the Tower of Babel. A common language unites; multilingualism divides! Your work undermining the English language in the U.S. is commendable, but you must increase your efforts lest the Americans wake up and realize what is happening. We recently received a glowing report about your efforts in the U.S. We received information that the following has occurred:

- There's a federal law requiring states and counties to print ballots in foreign languages and now it's done at over 1000 polling places in the U.S.
- A teacher was recently fired in a Western state for requiring her students to speak English in their classroom. Most were speaking Spanish.

- The Equal Employment Opportunity Commission is now suing organizations, including the Salvation Army, who require their employees to speak English.
- Driver's licenses are offered in foreign languages in close to 90% of the states; some in as many as 30 languages.
- The Obamacare web site offers access to the site in 46 different languages.
- The average person in the U.S. who doesn't speak English costs taxpayers an extra $150,000 over their lifetime.
- In health care alone, it is estimated multilingual services cost Americans $267 Million a year.

As you well remember, one of the strengths of America in the past has been that all immigrants and their children made a priority of learning English in order to become fully integrated into the U.S. culture. We must continue to convince new immigrants that this not necessary any longer and that the federal government will force American society to adapt to being a multilingual society. As I've said before, balkanize America and we are on our way to bringing them down.

You must work harder to defeat these state and national efforts to make English the only official language. Keep Americans from realizing that English is spoken by more people worldwide than any other and that it is the language of commerce and air traffic control worldwide. Keep using the ACLU to convince Americans that Official English Laws are unconstitutional even though courts have already ruled otherwise. Push multilingualism as a "right" for all people. Encourage people to speak foreign languages in order to make English only speakers feel like outcasts in their own country. See how this will divide and weaken America? It's a beautiful plan. Keep up the good work.

Your Beautiful and Intellectually Superior Professor,

X

Luscious Academianut Ph.D.

Following is one of a series of letters intercepted by Dr. L. James Harvey. They are from a Professor of Deception at Perverse University in Hell and are sent to his former students who are in the U.S.A. working to tempt America away from its Judeo/Christian values. Dr. Harvey has edited the profanity out of the letters and presents them for your information.

Perverse University ™

Department of Deception
P.O. Box 666
Smoke City, Hades 66666

Home of the Fighting Red Devils

Wonderful Obesity

Dear Fatulence,

The statistics we've just received from up there have us excited. The National Center for Health Statistics (NCHS) has reported that now 32% of Americans are obese and another 32.7% are overweight by government standards. Fantastic! You're doing a fabulous job up there and may qualify for our "Tempter of the Year" award. There was a loud cheer here in the faculty lounge at P.U. when I announced the new statistics.

Nothing can help our cause in bringing America down more than to make the patients there fat, lazy, and sick. Obesity does all of these. We can kill off the energy and creativity of the younger generation by making them sedentary; absorbed with their video games, iPhones, and hi-tech devices. Keep them focused on their own pleasure and entertainment, and use the sex saturated American society to stimulate them to destructive premature sexual activity.

We've warned you about that wave of "Baby Boomers" that recently to retired. With the time, money, education, and experience they have available they could be of great help to the Enemy and his church, if we don't stop them. Fortunately, you've had success there too. Statistics show that over 38% of those over 65 are also obese and spending 50% of their leisure time in front of a TV set. Fat, lazy, sick, couch potatoes, that's what we want. We know obesity is linked to numerous health problems including heart and cardiovascular diseases, diabetes, osteoarthritis, some cancers, and sleep apnea among others.

By the way, make sure the Enemy's church doesn't catch the vision of how these "Boomers" can help them. Leave the Enemy's people mired in that wonderful idea we support that once they reach 65, they are entitled to retire to a life of pleasure and leisure. We sideline thousands of the Enemy's people every year with that idea. And don't let the church develop comprehensive programs for seniors that keep them fit mentally, physically, and spiritually. These "Boomers" can hurt us badly if we don't stop them.

Not only does obesity rob people of energy and create health problems but it will place an increasing burden on the American healthcare system and drive costs way up. Obesity has been found linked to cancer, type 2 diabetes, heart disease and other health problems. Magnificent! Damage the healthcare system while you ruin people's capacity to be productive. I tell you our Father Satan is ecstatic that the long range plan we developed here at old P.U. is working so well.

You must keep the Enemy's preachers from mentioning being overweight is against the Enemy's teachings. Blind them to the meaning of the word gluttony and keep them away from biblical teachings like that horrid Proverbs 23:20-21 which warns Christians not to become gluttons. Make the preachers fear a back lash from their people if they mention obesity and gluttony, are sins. It's helpful also if some pastors, choir members, and leaders of the church are obese. That would be fantastic! They become living breathing visual examples every Sunday of what the Enemy doesn't want. This hypocrisy is delicious! Pardon the pun.

Set a new goal of 50% obesity in five years. "Lard up the Yankees" is our new motto.

Your Incredible Professor,

X

Luscious Academianut Ph.D.

Following is one of a series of letters intercepted by Dr. L. James Harvey. They are from a Professor of Deception at Perverse University in Hell and are sent to his former students who are in the U.S.A. working to tempt America away from its Judeo/Christian values. Dr. Harvey has edited the profanity out of the letters and presents them for your information.

Perverse University ™

Department of Deception
P.O. Box 666
Smoke City, Hades 66666

Home of the Fighting Red Devils

American Successes

Dear Americadown,

We conducted an exercise here yesterday and you would be proud of us. We decided to look at all the statistics we could find that proved our major goal of taking America down was succeeding. And what a list we developed. It made us proud of the work you and your colleagues have done and it makes us ultra-confident of our ultimate success.

As you well know, our major push to take America down dates back to the 1960s. That's when we won some major Supreme Court battles to throw the Enemy out of the public schools and public life. Roe v. Wade followed and the Supreme Court accepted that the founders of America intended to build a "wall of separation" between religion and government - something the founders never intended. All of this was supplemented by the great work of Alfred Kinsey, Hugh Hefner, Larry Flynt and others which eroded the sexual morals of Americans and ushered in the wonderful sexual revolution in the U.S. including unleashing our gay and bisexual friends and their campaign to make sodomy, adultery, and fornication acceptable.

It takes a while to turn a society away from its founding values, but we have made significant gains it in the U.S. in about 60 years. Our success is largely reflected in the data below. Read and celebrate!

LETTERS FROM PERVERSE UNIVERSITY

1. Since 1973 60 million unborn babies have been killed in the U.S.
2. The divorce rate has more than doubled and adultery is a popular indoor sport. A new study shows 70% of men and 50% of women cheat on their spouses. Fantastic! The American family is coming apart.
3. Over 600,000 Americans have died of AIDs and 1Million are now living with HIV.
4. One fourth of all children now live in households with only one parent.
5. Over 70% of black babies are born to unwed mothers.
6. The U.S. hasn't paid one cent down on its national debt in 67 years and their debt rating has been reduced for the first time in history. The national debt is now $30 trillion.
7. Sexually transmitted diseases have increased by 287% (based on # of cases per 100,000 people) since 1963.
8. Violent crime has increased 415.9% since 1963.
9. Test scores of U.S. students have dropped to 22nd in the world from near the top.
10. Gambling, once limited to Nevada, broke out in Atlantic City in 1973. Now 38 states have some form of gambling and all will soon have it. There are over 900 casinos in the U.S. and Sports gambling on ones iPhone is becoming epidemic. Gambling anonymous chapters are spring up all over the U.S.
11. Youth gangs called "Flash mobs" are terrorizing some U.S. cities crashing and grabbing goods, beating up innocent citizens, and acting like packs of wild animals.
12. Pornography is protected "free speech" and is saturating American society even in its elementary schools and public libraries with the approval of the American Library Association.
13. Gay marriage and bisexuality are widespread and are now protected by law.
14. Over 120 teachers in Atlanta, Georgia have been accused of helping students cheat on tests so they would score higher and qualify the schools for more federal money.
15. Americans now spend as much money on drugs as on education - marvelous!

The above data happily is only scratching the surface. We're on our way to taking down the U.S. Just make sure Americans do not relate the negative data above to the fact that they threw the Enemy out of public life including the traditional values of the Enemy which supported a moral society. Keep them believing they can build a successful society on the brilliance of man's intellect. Shield them from the many failures in history where societies have tried this and failed. Keep up the good work!

Your Brilliant and Attractive Professor,

X

Luscious Academianut Ph.D.

LETTERS FROM PERVERSE UNIVERSITY

Following is one of a series of letters intercepted by Dr. L. James Harvey. They are from a Professor of Deception at Perverse University in Hell and are sent to his former students who are in the U.S.A. working to tempt America away from its Judeo/Christian values. Dr. Harvey has edited the profanity out of the letters and presents them for your information.

Perverse University ™

Department of Deception
P.O. Box 666
Smoke City, Hades 66666

Home of the Fighting Red Devils

Kill Congressional Reform

Dear Congressdown,

While we have been celebrating your wonderful successes over the years in corrupting the U.S. Congress and the political process a serious danger is lurking of which we must be aware. Congress is spending America into financial chaos and hasn't paid down one cent on the national debt in over 54 years. America's debt of over $15 trillion is killing future prosperity. That's good and couldn't have happened if you hadn't corrupted Congress and the American political processes. But now we have a potential problem.

One of the worst and most corrupt lobbyists ever, Jack Abramoff, one of our most successful distorters of the political processes, came me out of jail some time ago where he had a terrible attack of conscience. You should have worked to prevent that! He has now written a book entitled "Capital Punishment" that provides a pathway for the cursed Americans to fix their political system. You must stop this at all costs! This holds the potential for undoing all your good work and for getting the American political process back where it was before all our wonderful corruption set in.

Here is what Abramoff suggested is necessary to cure Congressional corruption:

1. Eliminating all gifts to the political campaigns of members of Congress from any person or corporation doing business with the government.
2. Forcing members of Congress to live under the laws they pass for others. They now exempt themselves from most laws they pass. Put them under Social Security.
3. Prohibiting any member of Congress or their staffs from ever lobbying Congress for life, if they have ever been elected or served on Capitol Hill.
4. Instituting term limits for members of Congress - three two-year terms for members of the House and two six-year terms for members of the Senate.
5. Prohibiting "Ear marks" and keeping members of Congress from proposing, lobbying for, and for voting on projects in their districts or states.
6. Repealing the 17th Amendment and have senators elected to Congress by their state legislatures, as it was when the country began.

Do you see how this could destroy all the good work you have done corrupting Congress? You must stop any of these reforms from taking place.

One of the greatest dangers to our successes is to have those cursed Tea Party people get involved in pushing these reforms. The Tea Party people hurt us badly in the last election getting some of our friends thrown out of office. They have the potential to do us greater harm if they adopt a reform agenda and get any of the cursed recommendations of that turncoat Abrahamoff enacted. Work hard on this! Don't let it happen! I'll be watching you closely.

Your Highly Esteemed and Brilliant Professor,

X

Luscious Academianut Ph.D.

LETTERS FROM PERVERSE UNIVERSITY

Following is one of a series of letters intercepted by Dr. L. James Harvey. They are from a Professor of Deception at Perverse University in Hell and are sent to his former students who are in the U.S.A. working to tempt America away from its Judeo/Christian values. Dr. Harvey has edited the profanity out of the letters and presents them for your information.

Perverse University ™

Department of Deception
P.O. Box 666
Smoke City, Hades 66666

Home of the Fighting Red Devils

The Fluke Incident

Dear Truthtwister,

I can't tell you how much we cheered down here when we heard about the testimony of Sandra Fluke before Congress. You hit a home run with her testimony. Think of it, a law school student from the prestigious Catholic Georgetown University testifying before the world that she and other unmarried students are sexually active and not only that but they want the government healthcare program to pay for their contraceptive services. Fluke wants the American taxpayer to pay for her immoral behavior. Magnificent! We want that too!

The best part of all this is that, because there was such a harsh response from some of the Enemy's people to Fluke's testimony, President Obama, the president of Georgetown University plus 250 faculty, and numerous Democrat politicians jumped into the media to support Fluke placing them solidly behind her immoral conduct. How marvelous! It just shows how far down the slippery sex slope the Americans have gone. You were brilliant to drape the immorality in the clothing of women's reproductive rights. This tactic, which has won us some great victories in the past, such as winning support for sodomy under the rubric of gay rights, is brilliant. Americans are suckers for anything called a "right." We need to use this technique more often. Brand any sin we want Americans to engage in as a "right" and we'll have them begging society to let people have the freedom to do it. It's a shrewd strategy to get Americans to call evil good. Our Father Satan thought of it all by himself. He's brilliant, as we all know.

We also loved the Fluke incident because it set up the Republicans, who objected both to Fluke's conduct and request for free contraceptives, as opposed to women's rights. The more women who vote Democrat in the fall election the better for us. We must keep the Dems in power! We also congratulate you for keeping anyone, including the Republicans, from mentioning that Fluke's conduct was immoral and that, if the government granted her request, the government would be funding immoral conduct with the tax dollars of Christians and others who find Fluke's conduct reprehensible and contrary to biblical teaching. Getting the U.S.A. to fund immorality would be a major victory for us.

We are thankful for the support Fluke is getting from our liberal friends at Media Matters. They are opposing any conservatives in the media who support Fluke. Wonderful! Do all you can to help them.

Make sure you keep this issue alive and cloaked in the women's rights rubric. Do not let anyone in or out government define the morality of what is being requested. Our Democrat and liberal friends in the Christian church should be of help here. They are quick to dump morality for a "right" and for what is politically correct and popular.

Your Elite Professor,

X

Luscious Academianut Ph.D.

🔱 LETTERS FROM PERVERSE UNIVERSITY 🔱

Following is one of a series of letters intercepted by Dr. L. James Harvey. They are from a Professor of Deception at Perverse University in Hell and are sent to his former students who are in the U.S.A. working to tempt America away from its Judeo/Christian values. Dr. Harvey has edited the profanity out of the letters and presents them for your Information.

Perverse University ™

Department of Deception
P.O. Box 666
Smoke City, Hades 66666

Home of the Fighting Red Devils

The Bisexual Time Bomb

Dear Sextwister,

We think the time has come to explode the bisexual time bomb we prepared for American society. As you will recall, our strategy for destroying traditional morality in the U.S. was to get sodomy legalized under the guise of gay rights. The strategy was, of course, to get Americans to pass anti-discrimination laws and ordinances under the guise of protecting gays from bullying and discrimination. Our tactic, to use "sexual orientation" in these laws without defining what that meant, was a stroke of genius. Gays knew it meant sodomy and also bisexuality, but few, if any, passing these ordinances realized they included bisexuality and other "orientations." The genius of our efforts was to get liberal Christians and secular intellectuals to support these efforts without fully realizing what was involved. Some Christians will be horrified to realize that in supporting anti-discrimination laws they fought to legalize sodomy and bisexuality, which by definition includes adultery and fornication. In time we can use these laws to justify polygamy, pedophilia, and bestiality in the "orientations." Simply magnificent!

As you know, the group that helped us the most was the Lesbian, Gay, Bisexual and Transgender and Queer Community (LGBTQ). Your people knew, but never mentioned, that sexual orientation certainly meant bisexuality and it also even includes pedophilia, bestiality, polygamy and other sexual perversities. Most non gays including those who are liberal Christians never thought this through and thought they were only standing up for gay rights. It's time now to spring the trap and let them know they have opened a sexual Pandora's Box they can't roll back. We have a start with the ordination of a practicing bisexual in the United Church of Christ (UCC) recently. The UCC church that helped us so much with gay marriage and sodomy can now help lead the way to bisexuality and beyond. Logically we can now sweep all sexual morality aside in the U.S.A. because, after all, we are all born with a sexual orientation, which we have the "right" (boy, I love that word more all time, it has been a Satan send) to practice.

We must be careful in claiming our gains in the sexual area. Gently let the Americans know that bisexuals have the "right" to have sex with both males and females making sodomy a given and adultery and fornication their "right" in order to meet their needs. See the beauty of our time bomb. Without knowing or thinking much about it we got large groups of Americans and lukewarm Christians to legalize sodomy, adultery, and fornication. That blows the Enemy's morality right out of the water. Given the moral slippery slope we have the Yankees on I don't see how they can ever go back to their horrid Judeo/Christian sexual values, Tim Tebow notwithstanding. The traditional family is on the point of destruction. It is glorious to behold and you, Sextwister, and your cohorts should be proud of what you have accomplished. Our victory is near! Keep up the good work!

Your Brilliant and Humble Professor,

X

Luscious Academianut Ph.D.

P.S. We just got some great new statistics from a recent Gallup survey. The majority of Americans now believe it is acceptable for two unmarried adults to have sex and 54% believe it is acceptable to have a baby out of wedlock. This is great progress! The moral erosion hastens on!

LETTERS FROM PERVERSE UNIVERSITY

Following is one of a series of letters intercepted by Dr. L. James Harvey. They are from a Professor of Deception at Perverse University in Hell and are sent to his former students who are in the U.S.A. working to tempt America away from its Judeo/Christian values. Dr. Harvey has edited the profanity out of the letters and presents them for your information.

Perverse University ™

Department of Deception
P.O. Box 666
Smoke City, Hades 66666

Home of the Fighting Red Devils

Our 1619 Project

Dear Truthless,

Our 1619 Project is in trouble. You must rescue it by doing a better job of repeating the lies it contains. This horrible American writer David Horowitz has published a new book entitled "The Enemy Within" which exposes the lies our author, Nikole Hannah-Jones, put in the 1619 Project to promote the black race and promote racism in the U.S.A.

As you'll remember, Jones is a black left-wing supporter of Fidel Castro. The 1619 Project has been introduced into the curriculums of schools all over the U.S. and it has now been published in book form and is being sold nationally. We're turning young Americans and their parents into racists. We can't let this wonderful effort be overcome.

We're terribly upset that five of the nation's leading historians have signed a letter claiming the 1619 Project is full of errors. You must undermine them. Unfortunately, four are emeritus professors of history, two from Princeton University, one from Brown University, one from Texas State University, and one currently teaches history at the City University of New York all top historians from top universities. It looks bad when they claim our author, a former newspaper columnist, doesn't know her history. Since the five are all white and our author is black claim they are all racists.

I've listed and underlined the lies in the 1619 Project below so you can reinforce in all our soldiers what must be repeated over and over to create a false truth. After the lie I have listed the truths, which you must declare are the real lies. Remember our motto that a lie told often enough becomes the truth, if it is not forcefully contradicted. There's a growing effort to destroy 1619, so we must work harder. Here are the lies we must turn to truth and the truths we must claim are the lies.

1. <u>The Revolutionary War was fought to preserve slavery in America</u>. In truth it was fought to separate the colonies from the harsh and unfair governance and taxation of King George and England. It was fought to gain the freedom of America.
2. <u>The founding of America was 1619, when the first slaves came to Virginia</u>, In truth it was 1776 when the American British colonies declared their independence. Actually, the indigenous people in the U.S. practiced slavery long before this. Also, the first black slaves were brought into the Florida area in the late 1500s. Those who came in 1619 became indentured servants not slaves. They could earn their freedom by working off their debt. Actually, in the early years Virginia was a British Colony and there were no slaves' there, only indentured servants were allowed. Some indentured servants were also white and all earned their freedom in a few years after paying off the indenture through their work.
3. <u>It was the black slaves in America that were responsible for creating everything that made America exceptional including its economic, political, industrial, and other systems,</u> The truth is blacks were never more than a fraction of the population and were mostly slaves with limited power to impact the nation's development.
4. <u>It was blacks who won their own freedom and fought discrimination including helping pass the 13th, 14th, and 15th amendments to the Constitution.</u> Blacks never had this much influence. It was northern whites and Republicans who fought slavery and discrimination and established civil rights. Most civil rights legislation was opposed by Southern Democrats. It was over 300,000 male northern white soldiers

who gave their lives to end slavery. And a white male Republican President who abolished it.

5. <u>12. 5 million blacks were kidnapped in Africa and brought as slaves to America.</u> Actually, the number was far less, and they weren't kidnapped, at least by whites. According to the National Museum of the Royal Navy in Britain by the 1780s only 330,000 slaves had been sent to the new world and the British, the main slave traders, abolished the slave trade in 1808. In addition, the slaves were sold in Africa to white slave traders by other blacks, who had captured them in inter-tribal warfare in Africa. If kidnapped, it was by other blacks.

6. <u>Blacks created the abolitionist societies in the North and the underground railroad that helped slaves escape to freedom in the North and Canada.</u> It was northern white Christians mainly, who fought slavery from the beginning in the north and ran the underground railroad. It was whites who formed the abolitionist societies in the North and raised money to send freed slaves back to Africa if they wished to return. The African nation of Liberia so was formed.

Do you see how important it is to our cause to get people to believe the 1619 history is true? It undermines American history and creates a barrier between blacks and whites.

It gives blacks the credit for everything good in America and blames whites for slavery and everything bad that has happened to blacks. It opens the door for whites to pay blacks reparations and give them the right to enjoy affirmative action and other benefits to make up for the discrimination of the past. The 1619 Project can nicely be combined with our Critical Race Theory in the schools to pit blacks against whites. Forget and get rid of Martin Luther King's plea for judging people by their character not their skin color, we want America to judge all blacks and other minorities as victims and whites as bigoted privileged suppressors who need to make amends for their sins of the past. Just remember black is good white is bad. This movement has the potential to cause racial conflict in the U.S. and to further our cause of bringing them down. We can't let up, make our lies into the truth!

Your Fantastic Professor,

X

Luscious Academianut Ph.D.

🔱 LETTERS FROM PERVERSE UNIVERSITY 🔱

Following is one of a series of letters intercepted by Dr. L. James Harvey. They are from a Professor of Deception at Perverse University in Hell and are sent to his former students who are in the U.S.A. working to tempt America away from its Judeo/Christian values. Dr. Harvey has edited the profanity out of the letters and presents them for your information.

Perverse University ™

Department of Deception
P.O. Box 666
Smoke City, Hades 66666

Home of the Fighting Red Devils

Kill the Military

Dear Militarydown,

I was recently teaching Empire Demise 101 and was reminded how important it was to undermine the military power of important civilizations before we could take them down. Remember in Greece and Rome after significant achievements militarily they became soft. They began to use slaves and mercenaries to do their fighting and ultimately weakened themselves militarily to the point where strong disciplined and motivated enemies began to win victories and ultimately cause the empires to crumble. The corruption and immorality of the political system rotted these civilizations from the inside, but it couldn't have ultimately brought them down until the military was compromised.

We are delighted with the progress you have made in undermining the strength and fighting ability of the U.S. Armed Services. These services once the center of America's power and influence are now seriously degraded due to your actions. With women, gays, transsexuals, and illegal immigrants in uniform, force cohesion is being undermined, and political correctness is being worshiped in the military. You wisely used the Obama administrations obeisance to the radical feminists, and gays to force them into the military, which has had some marvelous positive results for us. Remember our motto regarding the military, "In diversity there is weakness."

The admission of gays and women has driven some of America's best officers to resign rather than officer a weakened military. They responded to Obama's famous admonition back in 2010 to, "get used to having gays in the military or get out." Some really good ones got out weakening the officer corp. And now the military is beginning to reap the whirlwind. Women in the military are reporting an increased number of sexual harassment cases and sexual assaults are sky rocketing. A recent study from the Defense Department indicated that sexual assaults in the military were up 50% in 2013 over 2012. There were 26,000 reported in 2012 and the Department of Defense estimates that for various reasons 80% of the assaults go unreported. Mix men and women together in close quarters at the peak of their sexual appetites and this could easily have been predicted. In addition, the number of unplanned pregnancies among the females in the military is booming in spite of the free contraceptives that are provided. Among women in the Navy 74% of the pregnancies are unplanned versus 49% in the general population. It's no wonder they now call many U.S. warships "Love Boats." It is estimated that each pregnancy costs the American tax payer about $10,000. I can't tell you how pleased we are that you have significantly undermined the effectiveness of the American military.

We were thrilled to hear recently that the Secretary of Defense said he was supportive of having transsexuals serve in the military. We wonder what bathrooms they will use <G>. They are also proposing allowing illegal immigrants to enlist. Will officers now be required to speak Spanish? We hope so!

More good news! While writing this letter I just received a news release from the Pentagon that made me leap for joy. The Pentagon says that 71% of Americans aged 17-24 are unfit for military service. They are either obese, lack a H.S. diploma, have drug convictions, or are otherwise mentally and physically unfit to serve. Wonderful! Soon the U.S. won't be able to defend itself militarily from its fanatic enemies.

You were a genius to use Obama's dislike for the military, his tendency to ape what the dying Western Europeans were doing, the radical feminists, and the gays all together to set the stage for the demise of the American Military. It has all come together beautifully and it is working wonderfully well. Trump tried to turn it all around but wasn't able to undue all the damage before he left office.

Now, we have Biden's Chief of Staff saying "white rage" is the military's biggest problem. He wants to drive all the conservative white soldiers out of the military because, he believes they are mostly Republicans who can't be trusted. Fantastic! More good soldiers will leave the services.

Keep the pressure on the military to open the doors to the Special Forces like the Navy Seals, and Army Green Berets, where women are still prohibited from serving. Make sure they compromise on the physical requirements women can't meet, as they have in the Marines already, so they can meet that wonderful goal of having "diversity" in the elite combat units.

We just heard that West Point has set a goal to have 20% of its student's women as soon as possible. I guess their football team, that is already finding it hard to compete, won't find any help there <G>.

Great work up there. We thank Satan for your positive results.

You Magnificent and Humble Professor,

X

Luscious Academianut Ph.D.

Following is one of a series of letters intercepted by Dr. L. James Harvey. They are from a Professor of Deception at Perverse University in Hell and are sent to his former students who are in the U.S.A. working to tempt America away from its Judeo/Christian values. Dr. Harvey has edited the profanity out of the letters and presents them for your information.

Perverse University ™

Department of Deception
P.O. Box 666
Smoke City, Hades 66666

Home of the Fighting Red Devils

Hyphenate America!

Dear Balkanize,

Your project to separate and divide the U.S. by Balkanizing the racial and ethnic groups is working wonderfully well. We're proud of you. We are particularly pleased with how you have encouraged the racial groups to hyphenate their references to themselves so as to create an assumed conflict with the Caucasian citizens of the country. When blacks refer to themselves as African-Americans they automatically say they are Africans first and Americans second. Hispanics do the same particularly the largest Hispanic group, which refer to themselves as Mexican-Americans. Never let them consider referring to themselves as Americans of African descent or Americans of Mexican decent. Make sure the African and Mexican are first and superior so the other Americans will feel the division that's implied.

Your main objective, which was to undermine the traditional objective of groups immigrating to the U.S., namely to integrate and become Americans, has now been eroded to become live separately in America as a distinctive and unique racial or ethnic group without integrating. That sets up wonderful opportunities for the separate groups to clash with each other and with American citizens who are proudly Americans first. We just received some great news namely that 61.8 million residences in the U.S.

speak a language other than English in their homes. Fantastic! Work to diminish English because a common language can be a unifying force and we thrive on divisions. We understand that most Americans when calling a major government agency or corporation in the U.S. are immediately asked whether they want to speak in English or Spanish. Marvelous! We also understand there are major cities in the U.S. like Miami and Los Angeles where a person can't get along in parts of the city unless they speak Spanish. Wonderful! This all leads to division and informs Hispanics that they don't need to learn English to live in the U.S. Having governmental agencies publish public documents in several foreign languages helps also. Anything that will keep people from integrating into that hated U.S. society is helpful to us.

I personally want to congratulate you on how you've use the George Floyd case and the shooting in Ferguson Missouri to inflame racial tensions. Be sure you keep Al Sharpton and Jessie Jackson, both supposed ministers of the Enemy, working to fan the flames of racial tensions. Keep driving a wedge between African Americans and other Americans. It's beautiful to behold.

We can also now use that wonderful Critical race Theory (CRT) to force racial groups to think about themselves and how they are discriminated against by the evil white majority in the U.S.A.

Keep up the great work!

Your Magnificent and Brilliant Professor,

X

Luscious Academianut Ph.D.

Following is one of a series of letters intercepted by Dr. L. James Harvey. They are from a Professor of Deception at Perverse University in Hell and are sent to his former students who are in the U.S.A. working to tempt America away from its Judeo/Christian values. Dr. Harvey has edited the profanity out of the letters and presents them for your information.

Perverse University ™

Department of Deception
P.O. Box 666
Smoke City, Hades 66666

Home of the Fighting Red Devils

The "Me" Generation

Dear Egotrip,

I'm writing to complement you on your efforts to separate Americans from any relationship with the Enemy and to lead them to that blessed state where they become totally self-focused on making a god of self. Some in the U.S.A. are even calling the millennials the "Me" generation in recognition of their glorious self-centeredness. You learned well the lesson I taught in my course Deception 201. You may remember I even used a reference from the Enemy's horrid book to help set our goals and vision for how to take down the U.S.A. In Judges 21:25 we read "Every man did what was right in his own eyes." The Israelites, in effect, rejected the Enemy and did whatever they wanted. The default position in humans is to make a god of self, if they do not believe in the Enemy or a supreme being. When this occurs hedonism inevitably follows and we have them for ourselves.

We laughed down here at a couple of examples of your success in the U.S. One was that woman, Rachael Dolezgal, who has passed herself off as a black person even though she is Caucasian. She even worked her way into a position of leadership in the NAACP. She, in effect, decided she wanted to be a black person and so she felt free to lie about herself. We also have that example of Bruce Jenner, the Olympic decathlon champion, who decided to become a woman. You also have that wonderful transgender movement in the U.S.A. supported by our gay friends reinforcing the fact that people based on their feelings can be whoever they want to be without regard to how they were created or formed. This denies the Enemy's teaching that he created humans as males and females. All of this helps us because it focuses decisions about sex and existence on how a person feels, and the self, not on the Enemy, his horrid book, or even on nature and creation.

Much of your success in making Americans totally self-centered and pleasure-centered have, of course, resulted because your fellow soldiers and former P.U. students have been so successful in separating the U.S.A. from its heritage and former reliance on the Enemy. The ACLU, atheists, gays, Freedom from Religion Society, secular humanists, along with a wonderful assist from the Supreme Court along the way, have pretty much driven the Enemy out of public institutions and life. We still have work to do, however, make sure our gay friends continue their assault on the Christians in America. Make sure they continue to believe they will never have the full acceptance and recognition in society they desire until the Christians are totally neutralized and compromised. We're winning! Another recent poll showed over 70% of Americans believes American morals are in decline. That's due to the good work you and your fellow P.U. alumni are doing. Keep it up!

Your Brilliant Genius Professor,

X

Luscious Academianut Ph.D.

Following is one of a series of letters intercepted by Dr. L. James Harvey. They are from a Professor of Deception at Perverse University in Hell and are sent to his former students who are in the U.S.A. working to tempt America away from its Judeo/Christian values. Dr. Harvey has edited the profanity out of the letters and presents them for your information.

Perverse University ™

Department of Deception
P.O. Box 666
Smoke City, Hades 66666

Home of the Fighting Red Devils

Go Secularism!

Dear Nationdown,

We have some good news and bad news to report. New figures regarding the religious affiliation of those in the U.S. is great. Those reporting "none" when asked their religious affiliation is at an all-time high, nearing 43% which is up from just 10% in 1990. That makes secularism and "non-religion" the fastest growing religion in America <G>. Fantastic! And among the younger generation of millennialists the figure is even higher at 48%. We've got America following the pattern we established in Europe where now 50% of the British and 40% of the Dutch report they have no religious affiliation and these figures are growing. We're winning and must keep up the momentum.

The bad news, I alluded to above, is that our reasons for being so successful in divorcing many Americans from their faiths is being exposed. By being exposed it allows some of our enemies to develop processes by which to counter our successes.

One of our supporters in the U.S., a Dr. Phil Zuckerman, the leading secularist in the U.S., has written a book entitled "Living the Secular Life." In the book he outlines the wonderful victories they are having in the U.S. but he also lists why we're winning and in so doing he exposes the reasons we have been successful. You must do everything possible to undermine his book and cover up his exposure of our strategy. You must read and then do your best to destroy this book.

He states in his book that we are winning because of five basic principles at work in the U.S.:

1. The conflict within the Christian church between the fundamentalists and liberals is causing some members to get fed up and leave the church altogether.

2. The sexual scandals within the Roman Catholic Church have caused many to sour on religion and leave the church.

3. The dramatic increase of women in the workforce. Women have traditionally been more important than fathers in passing on religious values to children. When women work this function is undermined. In Denmark and Sweden where they have the highest percentage of women working outside the home in the world, they also have the lowest levels of church attendance of any countries in the world. Encourage more women to work and we undermine their religious faith – marvelous! In the U.S. get the women to work and let the government take over raising the children. It's a winner for us.

4. The acceptance of sodomy and homosexuality undermines biblical Christianity, causes conflict in churches and denominations, and drives people out of the church. It has been a winner for us – keep it up!

5. The internet not only is using up time Christians might otherwise use in faith activities but it is presenting Christians with arguments and lifestyles that tempt them away from their faith.

Now, we must keep encouraging the application of these 5 elements, but we must cover up their existence lest some Christian evangelists use them to warn their followers thus causing them to avoid falling into our traps. Be warned and do everything to strengthen our efforts to undermine the faith of Americans.

Your Brilliant and Gifted Professor

X

Luscious Academianut Ph.D.

P.S. Now that the I-Phone has become ever present, keep people's attention buried in their phones playing games and being entertained and away from other more important things including friends and significant others, and especially the Enemy.

Perverse University ™

Department of Deception
P.O. Box 666
Smoke City, Hades 66666

Home of the Fighting Red Devils

American Betrayal

Dear Nationerosier,

We were recently made aware that an American author has published a book that exposes Father Satan's successes in undermining the character and values of the American government. We can't afford to have our methods exposed. The book authored by Diana West and entitled "American Betrayal" outlines in clear facts how the American government beginning in the late 1930s began to surrender the founding values of the U.S.A. and started using deception and untruths to maintain power and authority. West also points out how we used communists and communist sympathizers in government positions to undermine the American commitment to truth and integrity in national affairs. She also shows in detail how America's alliance with Joseph Stalin and the Soviet Union in World War II led us to compromise America's principles and values.

West outlines a number of major issues which hurt us and exposed how we undermined the values and character of the U.S. For example:

1. She shows how Stalin lied to the U.S. about the massacre of 20,000 Polish officers in the Katyn Forest in 1940. Stalin said the Germans murdered them and for decades the U.S. told the world they believed Stalin. Even though the Pentagon knew in 1945 that the Russians had

done it. Then the facts gradually came out and in 1990 the Russians had to admit that they had slaughtered a generation of bright young Polish leaders in cold blood. The U.S. Government had lied to cover for a murderous dictator.

2. Stalin promised that after the war he would allow the Eastern European countries to allow exiled leaders to return and establish their pre-war democratic governments. Instead, Stalin established communist dictatorships in every one of these countries and killed or jailed returning leaders who opposed his appointees. America did nothing to stop this and Stalin's agreements were turned into lies. America's good character lost again.

3. In the Yalta Agreement Stalin agreed to return to the U.S. all those American war prisoners who had been held by the Germans in camps liberated by the Russian Army. The U.S. had reason to believe there were at least 20,000 Americans so held. In return the U.S. agreed to return to the Russians all those U.S. captured Eastern Europeans who had joined the German Army to fight against the Soviets because they hated them more than the Germans. The U.S. kept its part of the bargain and sent thousands of these soldiers to Russia where they were either sent to slave labor camps or killed. Stalin told Roosevelt that they only held 17 Americans. The U.S. had evidence that Stalin lied, but did nothing leaving thousands of American Military to be killed or sent to slave labor camps to work and die. The American government covered up the reality (and is doing so to this day), and Stalin made the U.S., its word, and government look foolish and unprincipled. Even Boris Yeltsin later admitted the Russians had kept American prisoners. The American principle of never leaving a comrade in arms behind was surrendered and American character took a hit just as Father Satan desired. Even President Eisenhower, who commanded these soldiers at one time, did nothing to rescue them. Father Satan won again.

History has shown that during the late 1930s and WW II time period about 500 of our communist friends and sympathizers held key positions in the U.S. government including Harry Hopkins, Franklin Roosevelts top adviser, and Alger Hiss the Russian's top spy. These friends of Father Satan helped influence the U.S. to make a number of bad decisions, surrendering its integrity to the Soviets at times, and further eroding the Judeo/Christian values that had been the hallmark of American government before this. The surrender of the character of the U.S. to this day has followed the pattern of cover up, dishonesty, and lack of principle, the events listed above started. We must protect our gains. Do everything you can to destroy the value of the book mentioned above and also do all you can to keep the Americans in the dark about the true history of WW II and the years immediately thereafter. Make sure America forgets how it surrendered its values and character.

Your Incomparable and Irreplaceable Professor,

X

Luscious Academianut Ph.D.

Following is one of a series of letters intercepted by Dr. L. James Harvey. They are from a Professor of Deception at Perverse University in Hell and are sent to his former students who are in the U.S.A. working to tempt America away from its Judeo/Christian values. Dr. Harvey has edited the profanity out of the letters and presents them for your information.

Perverse University ™

Department of Deception
P.O. Box 666
Smoke City, Hades 66666

Home of the Fighting Red Devils

Censorship

Dear Truthtwister,

Your hard-won victories in getting the major social media platforms to censor Christian and conservative thoughts and ideas are now threatened by an initiative by the Christian Religious Broadcasters (NRB). You have been so successful in getting Facebook, Twitter, Google, and Apple to use their secular and atheistic value systems and algorithms to edit and censor conservative and Christian viewpoints in all their communication platforms that the Enemy's people are revolting and are trying to force our friends to be fair and unprejudiced in their content. You must stop them!

The social media is too important to us to lose our advantage there. This is where we shape the values of Americans, particularly the young, where we have been having such success. We've made great gains among the millennials. Over 40% now state that they have no religious preference. We can't let anything threaten these gains as we begin the battle for the hearts and minds of the generation Zers. Thank badness that most of the people working at these social media organizations come from the ultra-liberal Silicon Valley of California where conservatives and Christians are few and far between and those who are there are ostracized and persecuted.

As you may know, the NRB has established a website called internetfreedomwatch.org (even the name makes me sick to my stomach) to help document cases where there is prejudice and to develop a list to present to the FCC and government regulators. The NRB already has a list of more than 30 instances where Christians and conservatives have been censored.

You must undermine their efforts. Make sure our friends in the social media make the case for their freedom of speech rights and condemn the right-wing efforts to muzzle them. Make sure our friends paint the NRB and their supporters as white supremacists, fascists, bigots, and religious zealots who simply want their false ideas spread about. Marshall the forces we have in the Antifa Group to picket NRB headquarters and disrupt any NRB speakers who try to present their position anywhere but particularly at colleges and universities. Free speech be damned!

Truthtwister, this is critical. You must get some of the George Soros funded liberal groups involved along with Antifa. This is all-out war. We can't let the Enemy's people win this one. We know that if the social content on the internet is open and free, we will lose the contest between ideas, as has often happened in the past. Keep the Enemy's people off the social media altogether if you can, and if not, at least preserve our friends right to select the kind of information, arguments, and debaters that appear on their platforms and present our views. Use their freedom of speech against them and argue that our friend's freedoms to present what they want is superior to that of the Enemy's people to be heard on our friend's platforms, even though they use public communications.

Your Magnificent Professor,

X

Luscious Academianut Ph.D.

P.S. We just found out that Brent Bozell of the hated Media Research Center has released a major new study which exposes the major media centers strong bias against conservative views worldwide. Do all you can to undermine this study.

Following is one of a series of letters intercepted by Dr. L. James Harvey. They are from a Professor of Deception at Perverse University in Hell and are sent to his former students who are in the U.S.A. working to tempt America away from its Judeo/Christian values. Dr. Harvey has edited the profanity out of the letters and presents them for your information.

Perverse University ™

Department of Deception
P.O. Box 666
Smoke City, Hades 66666

Home of the Fighting Red Devils

Killing America Recap

Dear Nationdown,

I thought this year end would be a good time to recap Father Satan's long-range plan for killing the U.S. and to strengthen our efforts where we are falling short. As you will remember from your time here at P.U., Father Satan believed our key to success was to divorce America from the Enemy and his horrid Judeo/Christian values. Our Father's long-range plan had several elements, as I'm sure you remember, but let me remind you. Here they are:

1. To fill the education system of America with secular humanists and lukewarm Christians and to drive the Enemy, Bible reading, prayer, the 10 Commandments, and the Christian religion out of the schools and all public institutions.

2. To fill the courts of America with judges who oppose the Enemy and who see the Constitution as out dated. They will then look to other countries and to their own reason and emotions for legal advice helping to further undermine the Judeo/Christian values.

3. To undermine the various Christian denominations, particularly those who are most conservative and evangelical, by placing liberal leaders and pastors guided more by emotion than reason in positions of authority

in order to gradually erode the horrid values taught in that hated book. Remember its emotional pastors who have led the movement to ordain gays in key denominations, which Father Satan knew would erode the inerrancy of the Bible and put the churches on a slippery slope toward our values. It has worked wonderfully well in the Episcopal Church, the UCC, ELCA, The Presbyterian Church USA, and we are close to closing the same deal in several others.

4. To gradually undermine the sexual values of American society with introduction of pornography and display of a pleasure centered value system where Christian sexual mores are devalued and personal pleasure, particularly sexual pleasure is pre-eminent.

5. To destroy the Roman Catholic Church (RCC), the largest Christian body, by filling the celibate priesthood with homosexuals who would then also commit pedophilia and ruin the church's witness and influence.

6. To champion a set of materialist values built on America's capitalistic system that would encourage a wave of national materialism and indebtedness that would eventually bring the U.S. economy crashing down.

Now, we have been very successful. The public educational systems from elementary through graduate schools are staffed largely by our people and are turning out students who are secular humanist "snowflakes" and atheistic America haters. The courts have been wonderful particularly the Supreme Court and the 9th Circuit Court. They threw prayer, Bible reading, the 10 Commandments, and Christianity out of the schools and large parts of public life and made sodomy and gay marriage the law of the land. John Shelby Spong, the Jesus Seminar folks, and other liberal theologians have pretty much destroyed the Bible and shredded it's inerrancy. We can also thank our LGBTQ friends for helping out in this area as well, as almost single handedly they destroyed the Catholic Church with their sodomy and pedophilia. Hugh Hefner, Larry Flynt, with an assist from the Supreme Court have flooded America with pornography and introduced a pleasure centered sexual value system that is destroying the American family as both men and now women seek new partners chasing a sexual utopia. And materialistically we have the U.S., its corporations, and individuals in the largest debt in history. You and your colleagues have done exceptionally well, however, we are being challenged and can't let up while so close to ultimate victory. Here are some things you must overcome:

1. Continue to smear Justice Brett Kavanaugh and see if our democrat friends can impeach him.

2. Make sure the United Methodists and others approve the ordination of homosexuals this year splitting them and reducing their effectiveness.

3. Defeat the attempts of the RCC to reform itself. This Bishop Morlino from Wisconsin has hurt us by calling attention to the "homosexual subculture" in the RCC and the "sexual depravity" they have tolerated, which is destroying them. It actually got so good for us that there were RCC seminaries that wouldn't admit students to study for the priesthood unless they were gay. Let's not lose this advantage. Smear Morlino!

4. Encourage liberal states like California to support the recreational use of marijuana and other addictive drugs and to pass legislation depriving Christian counselors and psychiatrists from practicing reparative therapy on individuals who are gay or sexually confused. We must protect our homosexual friends and the practice of sodomy.

5. Make sure the U.S. government continues its deficit spending driving up the national debt and reducing the value of every dollar in circulation. An economic disaster is inevitable.

Your Brilliant and Precocious Professor,

X

Luscious Academianut Ph.D.

P.S. Congratulations on getting Michigan, in the past a conservative state with a strong Christian population, to approve the recreational use of marijuana in the last election. This inroad in the conservative Midwest bodes well for our efforts to make pot heads out of all Americans.

Following is one of a series of letters intercepted by Dr. L. James Harvey. They are from a Professor of Deception at Perverse University in Hell and are sent to his former students who are in the U.S.A. working to tempt America away from its Judeo/Christian values. Dr. Harvey has edited the profanity out of the letters and presents them for your information.

Perverse University ™

Department of Deception
P.O. Box 666
Smoke City, Hades 66666

Home of the Fighting Red Devils

Bless the APA

Dear Familydown,

We were toasting an action by the American Psychological Association (APA) in the faculty lounge yesterday. APA is continuing its activities to help us break down the American family by promoting illicit sexual activity. We celebrated down here in 1970 when the APA agreed with it's counterpart the American Psychiatric Association, and removed homosexuality from its Diagnostic and Statistical Manual of Mental disorders. This was done under extreme political pressure from gay political groups, as you will remember. We have also cheered the APA efforts to get reparative therapy made illegal. This therapy directed at helping gays change their sexual orientation back to their biological birth identity is critical to our cause, because our gay friends must prove that their sexual identity is inborn and is not subject to change. The fact that some reparative therapy has been successful must be labeled as false and little more than religious bigotry.

Christian psychologists must be defeated in the courts where they are taking these attempts to silence them. This will be a tough fight because these psychologists opposing our friends are appealing to the first amendment of the American Constitution, which they say gives them both the freedom of religion and freedom of speech they use in reparative therapy. Help our gay friends "judge shop" until they find liberal secular democrat judges who will support our gay friends. You should be able to win the cases on the way to the ultimate challenge at the United States Supreme Court (SCOTUS). This final decision may depend on who the next supreme court appointment is and that will likely depend on the next presidential election, which is why you must do everything possible to make sure Donald Trump doesn't run for president again.

But back to why we are celebrating the latest APA activity. Their task force studying human sexuality is about to recommend that society accept the fact that all sexual activity between consenting adults is healthy and something society should approve of. Fantastic! They call it consensual non-monogamy, but it is adultery! Marvelous! This will lead to the decriminalization of all consenting sexual activity and promote the destruction of the traditional Enemy approved families we hate so much. Prostitution, adultery, polyamory, and polygamy would all be promoted as legal viable sexual activities. This, if accepted, would destroy the traditional family and do irreparable harm to the raising of healthy happy children. What could help destroy the bed rock of American society more than the destruction of the family? You're already well on your way to this with over 70% of black children and over 40% of all-American children now being born out of wedlock. Another recent study indicated that approximately 50% of all American children will never live together at any time with their biological parents. Terrific! As Father has often said, you can't build a successful society without a strong family base. Our job is to keep that from happening and the APA is one of our strongest friends in this. Promote them all you can.

Your Brilliant and Insightful Professor,

X

Luscious Academianut Ph.D.

P.S. Don't forget the good work the APA did in 1998 when they accepted the Rind Report which suggested that some sexual relations between adults and children are positive. This has opened the door to supporting court cases defending pedophilia. Real progress!

Following is one of a series of letters intercepted by Dr. L. James Harvey. They are from a Professor of Deception at Perverse University in Hell and are sent to his former students who are in the U.S.A. working to tempt America away from its Judeo/Christian values. Dr. Harvey has edited the profanity out of the letters and presents them for your information.

Perverse University ™

Department of Deception
P.O. Box 666
Smoke City, Hades 66666

Home of the Fighting Red Devils

Keep Blacks Democrat

Dear Truthtwister,

I previously wrote you indicating how pleased we were that the Democrat Party has ejected the Enemy from their considerations. A recent study has shown that the vast majority of white Democrats are non-religious. I've also written you about how much our cause was helped when Donald Trump was defeated in 2020. Now I'm writing to remind you that a Democrat victory is heavily dependent in the future on your being able to keep the blacks in America locked into the Democrat Party. In the past they have believed our lies that the Democrats are the only ones that can promote their interests, Trump was winning some of their votes by delivering them jobs, higher wages, redevelopment in the inner cities and promising more. We can't let Trump win ever again and win more of the blacks. Keep them voting Democrat as they have in the past. We need at least 90% to 95% to vote our way, as they previously have, to be sure the Democrats win.

To ensure our victory, you must keep blacks believing the four lies we've sold them in the past:

1. All Republicans are racist.
2. Democrats are and have always been the champions of civil rights.
3. The Democrat agenda best serves blacks.

LETTERS FROM PERVERSE UNIVERSITY

Blacks need the government's help to succeed in life.

Now to keep the blacks believing the above there are some truths you must cover up;

A. It was the Republican Party and Abraham Lincoln (R) who freed the slaves in America. One of the greatest abolitionists was a black, Frederick Douglass (R) who said, "Republicans are the party of freedom and progress."
B. Republicans authored and helped pass the 13th, 14th, and 15th Amendments to the Constitution guarantying black citizenship and all rights including the vote. 78% of Democrat congressmen and 63% of their senators voted against the 13th amendment and <u>every Democrat</u> voted against the 14th and 15th.
C. President Eisenhower (R) introduced and signed the Civil Rights Act of 1957.

The Democrats tried to kill it and filibuster it in the Senate.

D. Blacks have been held hostage for decades by Democrat political machines in several large American cities such as Chicago, Detroit, Philadelphia etc. yet still vote over 90% Democrat. We can't let them wake up!

You can see the problem we have. Fortunately, many blacks have been brainwashed by you and your soldiers before and hopefully won't see the truth before the 2024 election. Keep portraying Trump as a white racist and bigot. Down play the abortion and same sex marriage issues or we may lose many blacks who are strong Christians and believe the Enemy's horrid book condemns the killing of unborn children and sodomy.

As I said before, the 2024 election is critical for us. We must win. Control of the Supreme Court and maintaining our hard-won recent victories depends on it.

Your Brilliant and Courageous Professor

X

Luscious Academianut Ph.D.

Following is one of a series of letters intercepted by Dr. L. James Harvey. They are from a Professor of Deception at Perverse University in Hell and are sent to his former students who are in the U.S.A. working to tempt America away from its Judeo/Christian values. Dr. Harvey has edited the profanity out of the letters and presents them for your information.

Perverse University ™

Department of Deception
P.O. Box 666
Smoke City, Hades 66666

Home of the Fighting Red Devils

Push Hard Left

Dear Faithdown,

The current political situation in the U.S. gives us a wonderful opportunity to deliver a fatal blow to the followers of the Enemy. Use the Black Lives Matter (BLM) to further our cause. Hide Antifa and the Marxists behind the BLM banner because their methods and violence scare people, while the majority of Americans are sympathetic to the BLM. Also hide the real goals of BLM, which are not shared by most Americans. Hide the fact that BLM grows out of the Black Power Movement, has Marxist roots, that it is globalist, is Democrat, anti-religious, supports open borders, opposes home schooling, supports sanctuary cities, opposes school vouchers, is pro-abortion, is socialist, anti-nuclear family, and anti-capitalism They are also anti-police and favor defunding them. They support rewriting American history to undermine American patriotism and are behind the cancel culture movement to take down all statues and pictures of historic American figures. Most Americans are anti-racists and support BLM but do not know or support their political objectives, which we support. So, keep the focus on George Floyd and hide BLM's Marxist anti-American values.

BLM coincides nicely with the liberal left as represented by Bernie Sanders and Alexandria Ocasio-Cortes, who are also helping our cause by pulling the whole Democrat party to the left, which is essentially atheistic and secular. They also are having a strong influence on the younger generation, which is already moving away from the traditional Christian faith. We just received some wonderful information from a Pew study. An in-depth study of church membership between the years of 2007 to 2014 indicated those liberal lukewarm churches, we love so much, lost 7.3 million members, while those horrible evangelical churches, that believe in that terrible book of the Enemy, have gained 2 million in membership. Those are bittersweet statistics for us. We love the losses in the lukewarm churches, but hate the gains in the evangelical churches. We just also saw a Barna study that showed between 2000 and 2019 church attendance among practicing Christians fell from 45% to 25%. We're winning!

The growing strength among the Sanders/Cortes followers helps our cause. Their strong anti-American and globalist message helps move people away from believing in American history and its Christian founding principles. This group is criticizing the Constitution and the electoral process, particularly the Electoral College. They demean the rich white male founding fathers, many of whom were slave owners, and therefore morally incapable of designing a utopian society. They are, without saying it directly, indicating that a strong central government today is more capable of solving societies problems than is the framework of a republic the founding fathers presented in the Constitution, which leaves governing in the hands of a republic and the people. And this is the beauty in all of it, **the left wants to replace God and the framework the forefathers created with a large godless secular bureaucracy based on man's reasoning, not the Enemy's truth. It's making the government the god.** By the way, it's just a short step from this to a one world government, which Father Satan has plans to take over and rule the world. Keep supporting George Soros who is helping us immensely. He shares all our goals and the best part is he is a Jew, one of the Enemy's chosen people.

You must continue your successful efforts to get the colleges and universities to promote the left's agenda. The wonderful group of professors we have working for us can be of great help. We just saw a recent study that showed that of the faculty at one of America's leading universities, Harvard, only 1% contributed to the Republicans. Everyone else contributed to the Democrats. While we know not everyone who gave to the Democrats will be strong supporters of our agenda, most will, and they'll make it hard for any professor to oppose us openly because their career may be at risk in that kind of environment. Keep up the good work and encourage all those in positions of authority to push the political system in the USA to the left.

Your Exceptionally Brilliant Professor,

X

Luscious Academianut Ph.D.

P.S.#1—The pandemic is giving our cause a boost as more and more Americans are looking to the central government with its money printing machine to bail them out of their financial problems. Use it all you can! Remember, kill the dollar and kill the U.S.A!

P.S.#2—Do all you can to stop the Durham investigation. I warned you before that this could lead to Trump's re-election, which we cannot allow to happen. Sabotage this investigation! Use all the dirty tricks and lies we taught you here at good old P.U.

P.S.#3—Keep that co-founder of BLM, Patrisse Cullors quiet. Even though she has resigned over financial irregularities, she recently told a reporter she was an anti-white Marxist. Hide the fact that her co-founder was also a trained Marxist.

P.S.#4—We just heard they tore down a statue of George Washington in Portland, Oregon, Fantastic! Just what we want. Destroy statues, change names, cancel American culture and get rid of American history. It's part of Father Satan's masterplan.

LETTERS FROM PERVERSE UNIVERSITY

Following is one of a series of letters intercepted by Dr. L. James Harvey. They are from a Professor of Deception at Perverse University in Hell and are sent to his former students who are in the U.S.A. working to tempt America away from its Judeo/Christian values. Dr. Harvey has edited the profanity out of the letters and presents them for your information.

Perverse University ™

Department of Deception
P.O. Box 666
Smoke City, Hades 66666

Home of the Fighting Red Devils

The Great Deception

Dear Truthtwister,

Our great deception is being threatened and you must increase your efforts or a great deal of our good work in the U.S. may be lost. You must undermine and crush this new book that is selling so well entitled "The Big Lie." How could you let that book get published? It undermines the work that we so carefully developed. We are in danger of having one of our greatest ruses exposed to the public with terrible consequences for our friends in the Democrat Party. You must smear the author, Dinesh D'Souza. Use our friends in the fake media to rehash D'Souza's guilty plea to having made an illegal campaign donation and his resignation as President of King's College over alleged marital infidelity. Do anything and everything to keep the American public from reading his book. It exposes our great deception, which has worked so well for us so far.

D'Souza has uncovered the fact that our condemnations of President Trump and the Republicans as racists, fascists, KKK members, and anti-black white supremacists is factually incorrect and in fact applies more appropriately to our friends in the Democrat Party that the Republicans. He has dredged up the fact that it was the Democrat Party in the South that supported slavery and withdrew from the Union causing the Civil War and over 600,000 dead Americans to preserve the nation. He has brought forth the facts that it was the Democrats that founded the Klu Klux Klan and forced segregation on the nation, particularly in the South, even after the Civil War. He also hurts us when he states that it was Democrats in Congress who fought and even filibustered to prevent the Civil Rights Act and the Voting Rights Act from passing and that it was Republican votes that passed those bills. Do you see how that hurts us? We've painted our friends in the Democrat Party as the great heroes of the blacks and civil rights movement and thus we have been able to secure 90% of the black vote for our Democrat friends now D'Souza is threatening to expose the truth that it was really the Republicans who have been the ones who fought slavery and voted for the rights of the blacks and minorities in America.

As Father Satan has said many times, if we tell lies often enough people will come to believe them as the truth. If the people are low information individuals, it becomes that much easier. We are now faced with the unfortunate circumstance that a high-profile, best-selling author and film producer, is publicizing the fact that Americans, and particularly black Americans, have been sold a bill of goods that is false. When you couple this with the fact that all of the disastrous inner cities in America have been controlled by Democrats it paints a horrible civil rights picture of our friends. This could lead to a back lash against us and our friends in the U.S. and Democrat Party. We can't let that happen. Do everything you can to smear D'Souza and keep him off all of the popular TV programs. Do not let him sell his truth to the public. If you can't stop this potential disaster for us, you will be recalled and disciplined. Do you hear me? This is serious and Father Satan is very upset.

Your Brilliant and Humble Professor,

X

Luscious Academianut Ph.D.

LETTERS FROM PERVERSE UNIVERSITY

Following is one of a series of letters intercepted by Dr. L. James Harvey. They are from a Professor of Deception at Perverse University in Hell and are sent to his former students who are in the U.S.A. working to tempt America away from its Judeo/Christian values. Dr. Harvey has edited the profanity out of the letters and presents them for your information.

Perverse University ™

Department of Deception
P.O. Box 666
Smoke City, Hades 66666

Home of the Fighting Red Devils

The Feminization of America

Dear Sexless,

We're really proud of your successes in emasculating the U.S. and making wusses of their military. This latest sex scandal in the Marine Corp is a wonderful move in that direction. Since the Marines were the one service that resisted most in putting women in combat, this scandal is likely to result in the alpha male ambiance of the Corp taking another hit. We're also thrilled at the continuing sexual harassment cases at the American military academies. As Father Satan told you, one of the ways to undermine the family and social strength of the U.S. was to undermine the role of the male father figure in the society. The Enemy intended for the father in a family to be the leader and perform the role as a spiritual leader building a Christian family, which is the strongest force opposing us. Reducing the male father figure helps us destroy the family. Our good friends, the American feminists, have helped immensely in their insistence that women are equal to men and can do everything the men do in the military. It is a lie, but it has been accepted by the wimpish military chiefs forced on the services under pressure from President Obama. Fortunately, you were able to hide from the Americans that the White House advisors to the President were mainly feminists. Obama's wife, Valerie Jarret, and Susan Rice constantly influenced the President to support the radical feminist agenda.

Under Obama the Pentagon became infested with gender equity wusses seriously compromising Americas' military readiness while serving their own political interests. You must keep that alpha male, Donald Trump, out of the White House or he'll role back all of our gains.

Be careful of this prominent feminist Camille Paglia. Her new book, "Free Women, Free Men – Sex-Gender-Feminism" is harmful to our causes. Even though Paglia is an atheist, and not one of the Enemy's followers, what she writes hurts us. She blasts feminists for never dealing honestly or properly valuing motherhood, which she says they have always played down. Paglia also blasts the movement to de-gender America by stating that science clearly proves that men and women are physically and hormonally different and that gender differences are biological and not changeable. In addition, she hurts our LGBTQ cause by stating, "…the idea that anyone is born gay is ridiculous….Homosexuality is an adaptation to social conditions." You can't allow leading academics and feminists to say things like that. She also states that, "…the DNA of every cell of the body is inflexibly coded as male or female from birth to death." This implies that it can't be changed and any attempts to cause gender modification are totally socially imposed and are contrary to nature. This hurts our cause. How could you let this happen? Get our friends to slander Paglia and to dismiss the book as anti-feminist.

Use the feminists push for equal wages in all positions between men and women to undermine the thought that there are differences in men and women. We want to use the fairness issues where ever possible to blur the fact that men and women are uniquely different and bring different capabilities to their tasks. Make sure the military services do not hold to strict standards for physical strength in combat related activities so as to allow more women to qualify. Remember we were counting on the fact that if scores of red-blooded men and women were thrown together in close quarters some sexual activities would take place that would lower force cohesion and help weaken the U.S. military. The U.S. military is now tied up with sexual harassment charges, rapes, and misconduct sapping its energy and reducing its effect as a fighting force. Your work is bearing real positive results for us. Any idiot could have predicted this would happen.

Thankfully the feminists were able to overcome common sense and force women into combat roles.

Your Brilliant and Insightful Professor,

X

Luscious Academianut Ph.D.

P.S. Make sure you continue to promote the toxic male superiority concept and hide the truth that the Enemy created men and women for different roles, but which have equal value. Confuse the value issue with the superior physical strength issue in order to fuel the radical feminist's fury.

Following is one of a series of letters intercepted by Dr. L. James Harvey. They are from a Professor of Deception at Perverse University in Hell and are sent to his former students who are in the U.S.A. working to tempt America away from its Judeo/Christian values. Dr. Harvey has edited the profanity out of the letters and presents them for your information.

Perverse University ™

Department of Deception
P.O. Box 666
Smoke City, Hades 66666

Home of the Fighting Red Devils

Flag Desecration

Dear Nationdown,

We are rejoicing here at old P.U. with the success you are having in making the flag of the U.S. a symbol of hate. Americans burning and desecrating "Old Glory" and failing to stand for the singing of the Star-Spangled Banner — how good can it get for us? Using that washed up black quarterback of the San Francisco 49ers was a stroke of genius. Now you've even got 8-year-old blacks, who don't even know what's happening, turning their backs on the flag in disrespect. The best part is they are allowing whites to believe blacks are unpatriotic and are supporting the destruction of American values and traditions. Do you see how easy it is to sow dissention in people?

When Colin Kaepernick decided to kneel rather than respectfully stand for the playing of the Star-Spangled Banner he set off a movement that is growing and expanding. You must get more black athletes in all sports to disrespect the flag. Drive a wedge between blacks and whites. Convince all blacks that the shootings of blacks by police are all racial crimes, and cover up the fact that the blacks who were shot were nearly all in the process of breaking the law. Make sure the whites are led to believe that blacks create an inordinate percentage of the crime in America and often resist arrest and incarceration. Let whites believe that blacks when they desecrate the flag are protesting American history, culture, values, and exceptionalism. This has fantastic possibilities for starting a race war and creating chaos in America. Never let the blacks realize how prosperous many blacks are or that blacks and people of color from all over the world are trying to come to America to better themselves. Also keep whites from admitting that there are a few bad cops and rare instances where they use excessive force. Keep the radical extremes on both sides from addressing the real truths here and solving the problem. Mix misunderstanding with some fanaticism on both sides to stir up the pot and lead to riots and physical confrontations.

Use the above issues, as you've begun too, to focus blacks and liberal whites on all the vestiges of slavery and the confederacy, which fought to preserve it. Have them seek to rip down all statues, flags, and symbols of the confederacy and undermine the historical validity of all Americans who either owned slaves or failed to oppose slavery all the way back to the countries founding. That would allow some to destroy the historical value of people like George Washington, Thomas Jefferson, James Madison and host of others. Do you see the beauty in this? We can undermine the history the Americans are so proud off and sow the seeds for a massive revolution that will destroy America. Propagate the big lie that American exceptionalism had nothing to do with the Enemy and his horrid values. This lie will allow America to go down that slippery slope into our secular humanism where individuals are gods and their selfish pleasures are the ultimate goal. When that ideology reigns, we win big time, as we have in countless civilizations before. Keep up the good work!

Your Handsome and Brilliant Professor

X

Luscious Academianut Ph.D.

Following is one of a series of letters intercepted by Dr. L. James Harvey. They are from a Professor of Deception at Perverse University in Hell and are sent to his former students who are in the U.S.A. working to tempt America away from its Judeo/Christian values. Dr. Harvey has edited the profanity out of the letters and presents them for your information.

Perverse University ™

Department of Deception
P.O. Box 666
Smoke City, Hades 66666

Home of the Fighting Red Devils

The LOVE Trap

Dear Loveless,

I'm writing to reinforce the importance of your use of Father Satan's love strategy in the U.S.A. You've had wonderful success in getting the U.S. to accept sodomy and gay marriage by distorting the concept of love, you must now use the same strategy to get bi-sexuality, pedophilia, incest, and polygamy accepted as normal sexual practices. As you will recall, Father Satan developed a strategy based on the fact that the English language has only one word for love. The English language does not distinguish between erotic love, family love, or an all-encompassing agape love. This allows us to hide our distortions of real love under one umbrella word for love covering up our real intentions. You wisely used this tactic to convince a majority of Americans that gay marriage was really an issue of allowing people to marry whoever they loved, totally covering up the fact that gay marriage involves the unnatural perverse sexual practice of sodomy. Thank goodness no one in the press ever used the word sodomy, which is the sin the Enemy hates so much. All of the Enemy's people approve of love, but most, when asked, do not support sodomy. And best of all no one ever made the case that two people of the same sex could love each other with familial or agape love without committing sodomy or needing to marry each other. Continue to make sure these thoughts never enter the minds of low information and liberal Christians lest we risk losing their support.

As you so cleverly carried out, you used the love concept to persuade numerous, mainly liberal Christians, to cave into the idea that gay marriage was just a matter of love not sodomy, and since love is good, gay marriage couldn't be bad. Now we must use the same strategy on our new goals. If successful, we can make incest, pedophilia, and bi-sexuality normal sexual practices allowing the American society to rot in a sea of sexual immorality that will make us proud here at old P.U. and guarantees our victory over the U.S.A.

Have our friends at NAMBLA (North American Man/Boy Love Association) argue strongly that pedophilia is no more than love between a man and boy and because it is love it is healthy and positive for both participants. Never let the discussion digress to what happens physically and sexually in the relationship, just that its love. Use the same approach with those involved in incest. Have them argue that it cannot be wrong for two consenting individuals to express their love physically, even if they are in the same family. Why shouldn't a mother or father have sex with one of their children since they are just expressing a deeper love for the child? Let the love argument over ride the sexual perversion and consequences of this behavior. I believe we can even get some low information Christians to support us even on incest as long as we focus on love, because in their stupidity, they will equate love with the Enemy and believe that love must be good in any circumstance.

Do you see the fantastic possibilities we have to take down the Americans? Push hard to get the U.S. to agree that some people are born bi-sexual. Use the same lie we got them to accept that gays are born that way and can't change. If bi-sexuals can't change then society must accept they should be allowed to have sex with both men and women in order to live a healthy sex life. If one accepts this idea, then society cannot in good conscience prohibit a bi-sexual from marrying at least two people, one of each sex, and there you have the unimpeachable argument for polygamy. See how it all fits together?

We're winning! Keep the Americans loving each other our way <G>.

Your Brilliant and Horney Professor,

X

Luscious Academianut Ph.D.

LETTERS FROM PERVERSE UNIVERSITY

Following is one of a series of letters intercepted by Dr. L. James Harvey. They are from a Professor of Deception at Perverse University in Hell and are sent to his former students who are in the U.S.A. working to tempt America away from its Judeo/Christian values. Dr. Harvey has edited the profanity out of the letters and presents them for your information.

Perverse University ™

Department of Deception
P.O. Box 666
Smoke City, Hades 66666

Home of the Fighting Red Devils

The Cake Court Cases

Dear Courtdown,

How could you have let this happen? You let the U.S. Supreme Court (SCOTUS) hand us a 7-2 defeat and a serious setback on the Jack Phillips cake baking case from Colorado. This is a serious defeat in our attempts to get government agencies and laws to override biblical teaching and Christian beliefs about sodomy. As you well know, our strategy has been to use civil rights laws with sexual orientation add-ons as a critical element to strike down the rights of Christians to use their first amendment religious rights to discriminate against homosexuals and sodomy. Father Satan himself devised the strategy. Its brilliant because it uses the American law and legal system to determine that sodomy is legal and acceptable which contradicts the Christians' horrid book which condemns sodomy. The beauty of the strategy is we have the U.S. law and government saying the Bible is wrong and discriminates against gays. This in turn undermines Christian teaching gives liberal Christians the ammunition they need to disregard the Bible as being infallible and puts at risk all of its teachings including those regarding Christ and that horrible atoning work he claims. Father Satan sees this as our great opportunity to subvert Christianity in the U.S. and to use the government as a tool to force our values on the nation.

We must increase our efforts on this front. We cannot let the enemy's legal forces win these victories.

We are thrilled that you encouraged a transgendered individual to go after Phillips again because he would not bake a cake celebrating her transition. The LGBTQ community that lost the last case has jumped on this one and the Colorado Civil Rights Commission, that was admonished for criticizing Phillips's religion before, are looking for a chance to get even with Phillips because they lost the last case. This case may get to the Supreme Court again. No matter what happens the court cases have disrupted Phillips's life for over 8 years already. You've virtually ruined his life because he believes in the Enemy. Great! Not many Christians will risk that. We'll win by being nasty and underhanded, which is our best strategy.

Be careful, however, we don't want to lose again at the SCOTUS. Trump's appointments might cause us to lose. See if you can get Phillips to withdraw the case. Try and bribe him if you can.

As you know, Biden will now nominate a new Justice on SCOUTUS since Justice Breyer resigned. He says he will appoint a black woman, which violates the civil rights law. Make sure he gets his way. A typical black woman will be just the kind of radical left-wing judge who will further our causes. See if you can revive the Democrat legislation to pack SCOTUS so we will have the power there to help destroy our enemies and make it impossible for the Enemy and his people to ever win a case there again.

Your Uniquely Brilliant Professor,

X

Luscious Academianut Ph.D.

LETTERS FROM PERVERSE UNIVERSITY

Following is one of a series of letters intercepted by Dr. L. James Harvey. They are from a Professor of Deception at Perverse University in Hell and are sent to his former students who are in the U.S.A. working to tempt America away from its Judeo/Christian values. Dr. Harvey has edited the profanity out of the letters and presents them for your information.

Perverse University ™

Department of Deception
P.O. Box 666
Smoke City, Hades 66666

Home of the Fighting Red Devils

Kill Christianity

Dear Religiondown,

Father Satan wants you to increase your efforts to destroy Christianity as a moral force in the U.S. As you will remember from your classes here at P.U., we taught that democracy, as practiced in the U.S., depends on its people having a level of morality for it to succeed. People must be willing to work together, to solve problems in a state of love, comity and compromise. We taught you that nearly all the leaders of the founding of the U.S., including George Washington in his farewell address, said that democracy can only thrive with a moral people with a religious foundation. That's why they added the freedom of religion as a critical right in the first item in their horrid Bill of Rights. Father Satan in his wisdom, however, said, that in the way the U.S. stated this right, they left the door open for us to undermine them and make our religion (atheism/secularism) America's religion.

The problem Father Satan found was, that the Americans in their attempt to avoid the church/state problems in Europe, wanted to avoid creating a state church in America so they stated all religions would be included in this freedom of religion. At the time 90% of Americans were Christians of various denominations and persuasions. The fact that the government was not to favor any church or denomination over another was even written into the Constitution, which also prohibits there being any religious test for government employees. Everyone at the time understood what the founders were intending to do in the language they used, however, Father Satan found a way to undermine them. Technically the way the language reads the U.S. government is separated from religious practice and stands above all religions just allowing all of them to be practiced, not favoring one over another, but assuming the vast majority would be Christian. Now 244 years later there are many other religions even including atheism, as the Supreme Court (SCOTUS) has ruled. Do you see the wisdom now in Father Satan's strategy to use the freedom of religion of non-Christians to destroy all the Christian values, and its symbols and religious beliefs that have permeated America since its founding? We essentially sold them on the idea that the freedom of religion right protected everyone from being influenced to practice one religion or another and essentially meant Americans should be freed from religion also. We used this effectively to get the 10 Commandments, prayer, and Bible reading thrown out of the public schools and buildings of America. We now must work harder to get everything Christian and religious thrown out of public life to preserve the freedom of Moslems, Buddhists, Hindus, and others to practice their faiths. We can soon, if we do this right, have all these religions in conflict with each other thereby creating internal conflict and weakening the U.S. In essence, we can get them to agree all religion should go, making secularism and atheism the religion of America. How great is that?

As you'll recall, Thomas Jefferson gave us a lift when one of his letters to a Baptist group in New England used the image of the U.S.A. having a "wall of Separation" between the government and religion leading to a misinterpretation of what he meant. Jefferson always supported the premise that the moral foundation religion developed in citizens was essential to the success of democracy. He believed morality was necessary to have a republic. If you are successful, Religiondown, you will prove him and the other founders were right, but when we use their good intentions to destroy that foundation, we will destroy America and win the victory Father Satan wants so much.

Keep up the good work – destroy Christianity!

Your Brilliant and Precocious Professor,

X

Luscious Academianut Ph.D.

Following is one of a series of letters intercepted by Dr. L. James Harvey. They are from a Professor of Deception at Perverse University in Hell and are sent to his former students who are in the U.S.A. working to tempt America away from its Judeo/Christian values. Dr. Harvey has edited the profanity out of the letters and presents them for your information.

Perverse University ™

Department of Deception
P.O. Box 666
Smoke City, Hades 66666

Home of the Fighting Red Devils

Killing Christians

Dear Truthtwister,

Father Satan wanted me to write to inform and advise you about a massive new push to undermine the Enemy's people in the U.S.A. We want you to immediately schedule a series of workshops all over the country for your soldiers in sin who are responsible for tempting individual Christians away from their faith and the Enemy. Father Satan put together a group of our brightest professors here at P.U. He tasked them with coming up with a list of things our soldiers in the U.S. could use as guidelines to achieve the greatest results possible in tempting Christians away from their faith, which is necessary before we can take America down. As we've discussed before, America won't fall until we take down the Christians and Christian churches that still believe in the teachings of the Enemy in that cursed book.

The P.U. faculty committee developed a wonderful list of priorities for our soldiers to follow in their fight to take individual Christians down. You are to teach these principles to every soldier working on individuals in the U.S. I have listed the basic principles below. Teach them in the workshops and then spend whatever time you have left to study some case study examples of how to use them and leave time for our folks to discuss what strategies have worked best for them in the past. This brilliant program has fantastic possibilities so expedite its implementation. Father Satan will be watching and wants continual feedback on its progress. Here are the guidelines:

How to Kill a Christian

1. Keep them from reading the Bible at all costs. No daily devotions or Bible study groups of any kind.

2. Challenge them to be dishonest. Take them down the slippery slope from slight exaggerations to gross exaggerations to white lies to real falsehoods and dishonesty. Tempt them to use President Trump as an example of how best to use exaggerations.

3. Tempt them into materialism. Lead them into wanting more and more.

4. Fill their minds with doubt particularly about the future, the afterlife, the resurrection, and about the inerrancy of the Enemy's book. Convince them the Bible is wrong about sodomy and once they believe that other errors become easy targets including the resurrection. This will also open them to conflicts within their churches.

5. Convince them there is no Hell and that a loving Enemy would never condemn anyone to an eternal punishment so horrible.

6. Confuse their thinking. Fill their minds with the latest fads in religion. Get them to believe all roads lead to heaven and a happy afterlife, if they just do a little good now and then.

7. Tempt them to sin. Sexual sins have always been our best weapons. A little pornography will help and the sex saturated American media will support us.

8. Keep them from praying at all costs. This could lead the Enemy to send individual help to them. If they must pray, make sure they do not kneel or pray in private.

Isn't this a brilliant list? Our faculty here at P.U. are some of the brightest minds in Hell. Good luck in implementing this plan. Father Satan has great hopes that this will tip the balance in the U.S.A. and we will finally have the conclusive victory we have been working for.

Your Diligent and Brilliant Professor,

X

Luscious Academianut Ph.D.

PS #1—We just got some great news from our people in England. A recent study there indicated that only 46% of the Christians there believe the Enemy's son died and rose from the grave. Fantastic! Over half of the Christians reject the heart of their faith.

PS #2—Good news from a U.S. study too. For the first time in history those marking "None" on a question regarding their religion outnumbered those marking "Catholic" or "Evangelical." Your good efforts are paying off. Keep up the good work!

PS# 3—We just got supporting data from a new Gallup survey showing church membership in the U.S. dropped to an all-time low of 50%. It fell from 70% in 1999 to 50% in 2019. A 20% drop in 2 decades. Wonderful! We'll soon have a working majority and then see the evil we can cause.

PS #4—Just a reminder that those churches and denominations that have surrendered the inerrancy of the Bible on the sodomy issue quickly slip into lukewarmness, the condition the Enemy hates most in his people. These people once they move in this direction are actually on our side. Don't harm them. Promote them and lukewarmness whenever you can.

LETTERS FROM PERVERSE UNIVERSITY

Following is one of a series of letters intercepted by Dr. L. James Harvey. They are from a Professor of Deception at Perverse University in Hell and are sent to his former students who are in the U.S.A. working to tempt America away from its Judeo/Christian values. Dr. Harvey has edited the profanity out of the letters and presents them for your information.

Perverse University ™

Department of Deception
P.O. Box 666
Smoke City, Hades 66666

Home of the Fighting Red Devils

Father Satan's Lecture

Dear General Tempter,

I'd like you to circulate this letter to all of your comrades there in the U.S. working to take the country down. Last week Father Satan came by to address our student body in our annual convocation. Our Father was his usual eloquent self. In his address our Father summarized the strategies we are using in the U.S. He keyed his address to a major pronouncement made by Mahatma Gandhi many years ago. While Gandhi wasn't one of the Enemy's people he did and said things, which hurt our cause very badly. In fact, his "six social sins" have been quoted far and wide across the world to warn people about what they must not do if their nations are to succeed. Father Satan turned it around and told our students that Gandhi had detailed exactly what we needed to do to bring nations down. I'm sure most of your colleagues will remember studying this here at old P.U., but it deserves to be repeated because it is so profound. As you will recall, Mahatma Gandhi said that the following "seven social sins" would bring any nation down:

1. Politics without principle
2. Wealth without work
3. Commerce without morality

4. Pleasure without conscience
5. Education without character
6. Science without humanity
7. Worship without sacrifice

Following our Father's lecture, the faculty and I had a session where we looked at each point and assessed how we were doing in the U.S.A. Next week we will do the same for our work in Israel, that other loathsome democracy that harbors so many of the Enemy's favorite people.

So, let me share some of our observations and suggestions. On number 1 we believe you are making wonderful progress. The U.S. political system is in chaos. The parties are fighting with each other and the Democrats are fighting within. Neither party is legislating in the interests of the people, and they haven't paid down one cent on the national debt in over 67 years, which has now spiraled to over 30 trillion dollars. On #2 there is a burgeoning class of billionaires who do little work and numerous hedge fund executives who are getting wealthy by moving other people's money around. We thought you should do more to promote corruption in the business sector. Corrupt it like you have the military Industrial complex. On #4 you have done a masterful job. Homosexuality is running rampant, fewer young people are not getting married but are still having sex, pornography is rampant, and America is fast becoming the Sodom and Gomorra of the 21st century. On #5 education you have also done well. You've thrown the Enemy out of public education and most of public life. There's no foundation left for them to build character. We've also warned you, however, the Enemy is undermining our world view foundation built on a godless evolution. This new science could lead to a move to intelligent design which could hurt us. Stop this movement at all costs! We face this danger in #6 science, as the exceptional discoveries in cellular structure, particularly in the DNA are leading more and more scientists to believe there had to have been a creator of immense intellectual capacity to create such a system. They can no longer believe it developed through random evolution. This possesses a great danger to us. You have done very well in #7. You have almost all major Christian churches and denominations in crisis and decline. You have done a masterful work in using the LGBTQ group and sodomy to split and weaken major denominations. The Episcopalians, Presbyterians (USA), the UCC, the ELCA, and the Roman Catholics are all in decline and losing members. And we have the United Methodists near a split. The ones that split, however, often leave a hard core of self-sacrificing conservatives that continue to serve the Enemy effectively and start to grow. Remember if you prune a tree correctly you free it to grow stronger. You must kill the tree. The weak liberal off shoots of these split denominations will wither and actually help us as lukewarm versions of Christianity. Let them be and help us. Work to kill the ones who continue to follow the Enemy and his horrid book.

Generally speaking, we think you're doing very well, but don't become over confident or we could lose these hard-won gains.

Your Eminently well Qualified and Brilliant Professor

X

Luscious Academianut Ph.D.

Following is one of a series of letters intercepted by Dr. L. James Harvey. They are from a Professor of Deception at Perverse University in Hell and are sent to his former students who are in the U.S.A. working to tempt America away from its Judeo/Christian values. Dr. Harvey has edited the profanity out of the letters and presents them for your information.

Perverse University ™

Department of Deception
P.O. Box 666
Smoke City, Hades 66666

Home of the Fighting Red Devils

Destroy America Conference

Memo To: All Devils Serving in the United States
From: Professor Luscious Academianut Ph.D.
Regarding: Destroy America Conference

Father Satan asked that I send this memo to share with you the results of our semi-annual conference on taking down the United States. Father Satan reminded us all about the 5 signs that preceded the collapse of the Roman Empire, one of our great accomplishments from the past. He then compared where the U.S. is on the same issues. As you may recall from your course Destroying America 101 here at old P.U., the 5 characteristics of a dying empire are:

An increasing love of affluence and a growing materialism.
A widening gap between the rich and the poor.
An obsession with sex.
A freakishness in the arts masquerading as creativity and originality.
An increased desire to live off the state

These are all described in Edward Gibbon's book "The Decline and Fall of the Roman Empire," which as you'll remember, we used in the course to help outline the way we were going to attack and bring down the U.S.

Father Satan reviewed our progress on each of these points, as I'll mention below, and summarized by saying He believes we have the U.S. on the ropes and near the full collapse that we have been working for. Father Satan mentioned the exorbitant salaries currently being paid sports stars, corporate executives, hedge fund managers, and Hollywood stars as contrasted to the stagnant wages of the lower and middleclass workers in the U.S. We know this breeds unrest and rebellion, if not corrected. We also see the rapid growth of pornography, adultery, homosexuality, divorce and sex outside of traditional marriage undermining the raising of healthy well-adjusted children. And regarding the arts we just saw an artist being celebrated whose art consisted of placing swing cans of paint with holes in them over a canvas allowing the splattering paint to form an artistic piece that people pay big money to buy. Also point 5 above is being illustrated by the increasing number of people becoming dependent on section 8 housing, SSI handouts, Medicaid and the increasing number of welfare programs. It seems some politicians lay awake nights trying to figure out new welfare handouts, like Obama phones, that that bought them more votes in the next election. And all this welfare in a nation with a 30 trillion-dollar debt and in October it will be 67 years straight where the Federal Government has never paid down one cent on the national debt. In addition, there are no plans to balance the national budget or pay down on the debt in the near future. This is called national suicide.

Father Satan warned us not to become complacent or over confident. The Trump administration, if he is re-elected, who talks about defending Western values, could still pose a problem. A spiritual awakening in the U.S. could still revive their faith in the Enemy and turn them back to the cursed values upon which the nation was founded. Fortunately for us this becomes less likely as we lead the U.S. down the same slippery slope, we took Rome down. Don't let up and we're assured to take down the greatest nation that ever existed.

Father Satan sends his best. Keep up the good work.

P.S. make sure you do everything you can to keep Americans from going to the U.S. Treasury Departments web site where they have recorded the historical U.S. national debt by years all the way back to 1789, when the Constitution took effect. Keep everyone away from the site because it proves the U.S. hasn't paid a dime down on the debt in 67 years. Also hide the fact that no current budget proposals plan any debt reduction for 10 years or more, piling more trillions in debt on future generations.

LETTERS FROM PERVERSE UNIVERSITY

Following is one of a series of letters intercepted by Dr. L. James Harvey. They are from a Professor of Deception at Perverse University in Hell and are sent to his former students who are in the U.S.A. working to tempt America away from its Judeo/Christian values. Dr. Harvey has edited the profanity out of the letters and presents them for your information.

Perverse University ™

Department of Deception
P.O. Box 666
Smoke City, Hades 66666

Home of the Fighting Red Devils

Media Madness

Dear Mediadown,

I can't tell you how happy we are down here to see how you have undermined the American commitment to truth and objectivity in journalism. It's fantastic to see some of the pillars of traditional journalism in America like the New York Times, Washington Post, NBC, ABC, and CBS publishing fake news from unnamed sources, which is untrue and intended to destroy former President Trump and the GOP. A renown journalist, Michael Goodwin, who formerly taught at the prestigious School of Journalism at Columbia University, recently said current journalism as practiced by these aforementioned media giants is a disgrace. He suggested that the 2016 election caused the practice of journalism to "have a Humpty Dumpty moment. It fell off the wall, shattered into a million pieces and can't be put back to gather again" (Goodwin quote from Imprimis, Vol. 46, Hillsdale College). Not only this but we now have a totally fake news group formed by CNN, MSNBC, and PBS, and PBS is funded largely through American tax dollars. What could be better for us – Americans funding their own demise with their tax dollars <G>.

We're delighted with your work and the potential this false news has for producing dissention and conflict within American society. One pundit actually, because of all this, said America is on the verge of a civil war. If you can cause that you're a lock on admission to our "Satan Hall of Fame." We laughed when we heard some American reporters are actually suggesting the major journalistic outlets have been stricken by a "Trump Disorientation Syndrome." Marvelous! Make sure your people stand strong for the fake news even when adversaries like Tucker Carlson, Mark Levin, Michael Savage, Shawn Hannity and others fire back with the truth. As our Father Satan has often said, "If you lie often enough, for most unthinking people, it soon becomes the truth." Sow the seeds of discontent in the U.S. and encourage more conflict like the recent insurrection on Jan. 6, 2021.

Feed the fake news machine and continue to help them focus on getting rid of former President Trump forever. Enough false accusations will produce so much smoke even some of his supporters will believe there must be some fire, even if there is none. Make sure any Trump supporters are denied the opportunity to speak on college campuses, and if they try make sure our supporters threaten force. Most college administrations are wusses and will find reasons to cancel such invitations to avoid any unpleasantness and extra security costs.

The bottom line is you have succeeded in compromising one of America's most important institutions namely its honest objective journalistic tradition. Americans now have their opportunity to read and hear the truth about current affairs significantly compromised. Our chance to spread fake truth and lies is marvelously enhanced. Run with that ball and cause all the dissention and conflict you can. An open civil war in the U.S. is a delicious possibility we didn't think was even possible a few years ago. Now it's a realistic possibility. Fantastic. Keep up the good work. Keep your eye on the great honor induction into our Hall of Fame would be.

Your Ingenious Professor

X

Luscious Academianut Ph.D.

LETTERS FROM PERVERSE UNIVERSITY

Following is one of a series of letters intercepted by Dr. L. James Harvey. They are from a Professor of Deception at Perverse University in Hell and are sent to his former students who are in the U.S.A. working to tempt America away from its Judeo/Christian values. Dr. Harvey has edited the profanity out of the letters and presents them for your information.

Perverse University ™

Department of Deception
P.O. Box 666
Smoke City, Hades 66666

Home of the Fighting Red Devils

Kill Charter Schools, Home Schooling, and Vouchers

Dear Eddown,

You've got to be more successful in killing off charter schools, home schooling, and voucher programs which allow American children to avoid our brainwashing programs in the public schools. We've spent a lot of time and effort compromising the teacher's unions, and putting in place curriculum materials, like the 1619 Project and our Critical Race Theory, that will brainwash American children to our way of thinking. Don't let our advantage slip away now that our Democrat friends are in power.

That horrid Secretary of Education under Donald Trump, Betsey DeVos, did our cause a great deal of harm. And that black Secretary of HUD, Ben Carson helped her push these horrid voucher programs through, which allow minority children to escape our influence in the public schools by fleeing to private, parochial, and charter schools with tax payer's money. Horrible! There are now 8.7 million American students in private and religious based schools. We can't afford to lose our influence on that many students. Change these trends at all costs. Father Satan gives this the highest priority!

Father Satan is furious that you have allowed West Virginia to become the first state to allow elementary and high school students to take their allocated state tax funds as a voucher to any school their parents choose including private, parochial, Christian, or charter schools. We must stop this movement. It threatens to undo all the good work we've done to win the public schools and teachers unions of America to our cause. You've also failed to stop the increase in home schooling, which has more than doubled in recent years and now involves 11.1% of American households. You're going to lose your job if you don't reverse these trends.

See if you can find some way to undermine this black intellectual, Thomas Sowell, he's hurting us as he pushes for voucher programs and keeps pushing forth data to show how they help minority students gain a quality education. We can't allow him to succeed in persuading the black community, particularly in the large black inter cities, to oppose their black Democrat political establishments, and their teacher's union friends, that keep the disastrous public schools true to our values. Kill charter schools and kill voucher programs! You must destroy all these studies that show that charter school and parochial school students routinely do better on tests of proficiency that do the public-school students. Also please do all you can to kill and disprove these tests that show American public-school students routinely score far below those of students in other countries of the world. That hurts our cause.

Now, you've got some help in destroying the Catholic parochial schools. The sexual misconduct of so many priests in the church has led to countless law suits, which is draining the church of funds. This is forcing their schools to either close or increase tuition that many families can't afford. They then must send their children to the public schools. We'll continue pressure from that direction, which should cause many more Catholic schools to close. We can't let them get public money through a voucher program. Do you see how that could hurt us? It's critical we kill this.

Continue to work with the teacher's unions. Keep them from wanting to open schools closed because of covid-19. The longer students stay out the more their educational development will suffer. Also make sure the teacher's unions require the schools to use the 1619 Project addition, which sows the seeds of white racism in the minds of the students and leads to that wonderful racial confrontation we want so badly. Divide America racially! Push Critical Race Theory. Balkanize them along racial lines and we'll weaken them beyond repair, opening the door for our marvelous one world government which we will control.

Father Satan can't wait until we make this happen.

Your Brilliant and Humble Professor

X

Luscious Academianut Ph.D.

Following is one of a series of letters intercepted by Dr. L. James Harvey. They are from a Professor of Deception at Perverse University in Hell and are sent to his former students who are in the U.S.A. working to tempt America away from its Judeo/Christian values. Dr. Harvey has edited the profanity out of the letters and presents them for your information.

Perverse University ™

Department of Deception
P.O. Box 666
Smoke City, Hades 66666

Home of the Fighting Red Devils

Ride Wokism Kill Loudounism

Dear Wordjockey,

We've got some words we've got to use more effectively in the U.S. to promote our cause. The word "wokism" is working well for us. It's being used widely and our supporters are proud to be woke and quick to condemn the Enemy's people who are not woke. Our people are proud to have been awakened to the white racism in America and the horrid foundations of the nation that were put in place by old white slave owners. They established everything American in order to favor the white majority in the country and to make slavery permanent. So, promote Wokism all you can. Make those who aren't woke feel ignorant and left out.

Now, we have a growing problem with the use of the words Critical Race Theory (CRT). We want to continue the teaching of all the lies inherent in this concept, namely that America is and always has been a white racist country which has discriminated against all peoples of color, but we need to change the name because CRT has developed a bad reputation. The Enemy's people have linked CRT to socialism, Black Lives Matter and its Marxist foundation, as well as to that atheist Harvard professor, Derrick Bell, who first brought it forth. They have so tarnished the concept that people are turning against it when they hear the name CRT. So, without changing the wonderful teaching of CRT we will change the name of the concept to Social and Emotional Learning (SEL). This sounds so much better and people will be fooled into thinking it is replacing CRT, which it is not. We're just renaming it. Sell (SEL). Got that humor?

Now, related to all this is something Father Satan is furious about. It's the terrible election loss we suffered in Virginia recently. Not only did our friend, Terry McAuliffe, lose but even worse the Republicans elected the first black woman, Winsome Sears, as the Lt. Governor. She's a loud-mouthed critic of the Biden administration and likely to hurt us in Virginia over the next 4 years. All of this likely was caused in part by a revolt against the school board in Loudoun County, Virginia over CRT and the boards stupid coverup of a student rape by a transgendered male in a girl's restroom. The parents have organized, fought the board, and their efforts have gone national encouraging parental groups all over the country to rise up and challenge CRT. The movement is so popular it's now being call Loudounism. It's hurting us. The parents have even formed a new legal group "Parents Against CRT" and they are going countrywide with it. Put a stop to this movement any way you can. It threatens all the progress we've made in the colleges and universities, as well as major American businesses and corporations, who have been buying into our CRT concept. Do you see why Father Satan is so upset? We can't let all the progress we've made to undermine American history, values, founding documents, and heritage by letting these parental groups grow and destroy CRT. Keep up the cancel culture and 1619 Project efforts and the efforts to convince white Americans that they should be ashamed of their history and be looking for ways to compensate all minority groups of color for the racism and discrimination of the past, which continues to the present day. We've come a long way in our effort to take America down. We can't let up. Go to work to change the language and help us win the ultimate victory.

Your Illustrious and Brilliant Professor,

X

Luscious Academianut Ph.D.

P.S.#1— Father Satan is thrilled how Biden is using the Department of Justice (DOJ) and the FBI to further his political purposes. We rejoiced down here when we heard the FBI raided the home of one of the parents leading the fight against school boards supporting CRT. The FBI and DOJ are in our corner use them! Make all parents opposing us domestic terrorists, so we can close them down.

P.S.# 2— Miranda Divine's book "Laptop from Hell" has been released – kill it! We can't let this book, which lays out all the criminality of Hunter and Joe Biden, educate the American public on the misconduct of the Bidens. Pull out all the stops – have the Bidens sue her! Do whatever you can.

LETTERS FROM PERVERSE UNIVERSITY

Following is one of a series of letters intercepted by Dr. L. James Harvey. They are from a Professor of Deception at Perverse University in Hell and are sent to his former students who are in the U.S.A. working to tempt America away from its Judeo/Christian values. Dr. Harvey has edited the profanity out of the letters and presents them for your information.

Perverse University ™

Department of Deception
P.O. Box 666
Smoke City, Hades 66666

Home of the Fighting Red Devils

Dead Churches

Dear Churchdown,

We just received some marvelous news from up there about another church that you have taken down. It is now a wonderful example for us of lukewarm Christianity. Recent data from the Church of Sweden indicates that only 15% of its baptized members believe in Jesus Christ. Another 15% say they are atheists and 25% indicate they are agnostics. Only 2% attend church with any regularity. This once vibrant Lutheran Church is currently dead. It now serves as an example of lukewarm valueless Christianity.

Your focus with other Christian churches must be to undermine their belief in Jesus and his resurrection. This is the cornerstone of their beliefs so undermine it. Our good friend Bishop John Shelby Spong did wonderful work for us in the Episcopal Church in the U.S. convincing many the Bible was unreliable and Jesus wasn't who he said he was. The Episcopal Church is hopelessly split, supporting the ordination of gays, and dying - a great victory for us.

Let me suggest a new strategy for you. There is a growing attempt to bring Moslems and Christians together to prevent religious conflict. Since Moslems accept Jesus as a prophet yet deny he was the son of God and that he died and was resurrected, we should pressure Christians to modify or give up their belief in Jesus' divinity in order to make peace with the Moslems. Do you see the beauty in this for us? Get Christians to give up their core belief in Christ and his salvation in order to gain peace. There's our Father Satan's favorite strategy again - get Christians to do wrong for a good reason.

The Yale Center for Faith and Culture has a project that can also help us. In order to bring Christian and Moslem leaders together they have issued a statement already signed by 300 Christian clergymen agreeing that Allah and Yahweh is the same God. This statement was signed by Rick Warren, and Bill Hybels among others. They are getting sucked in - do you see the potential here for us to get them to compromise basic Christian beliefs in the interest of making peace? It's a winner for us. Already we have heard of some Christian missionaries working in Moslem areas in Africa who have eliminated 91 verses in the Bible that refer to Jesus as the son of God because that is offensive to the Moslems. This is exactly what we want. Soon a watered-down Christianity will be like the Church of Sweden doing us more good as a lukewarm church than no church at all. Remember my recent letter about Solomon. The wisest man of his time was taken down and disobeyed the Enemy out of compassion for his pagan wives. Give even the wise patients of the Enemy a good reason and we can get them to do our Father's bidding. Ride that horse! It's a winner!

Your Brilliant, Attractive, and Humble Professor

X

Luscious Academianut Ph.D.

LETTERS FROM PERVERSE UNIVERSITY

Following is one of a series of letters intercepted by Dr. L. James Harvey. They are from a Professor of Deception at Perverse University in Hell and are sent to his former students who are in the U.S.A. working to tempt America away from its Judeo/Christian values. Dr. Harvey has edited the profanity out of the letters and presents them for your information.

Perverse University ™

Department of Deception
P.O. Box 666
Smoke City, Hades 66666

Home of the Fighting Red Devils

Kill Easter

Dear Faitheroder,

Our plan to drive anything related to the Enemy out of American life can't move forward unless you do a better job of getting rid of all the symbolism that links Easter to the Enemy and his son. Make sure all public schools replace references to Easter and replace it with "Spring Festival." Do not allow them to speak of Easter eggs rather have them refer to "Spring Spheres." If they must have an Easter egg hunt label it a "Candy Hunt using Spring Spheres." We must at all costs divorce anything in this season from that horrible defeat our father Satan suffered when the Enemy's son escaped us.

Make sure all references to a resurrection or springing forth are related to natures blooming in the Spring not to the Enemy's son rising from the dead. We can accomplish this under that wonderful guise of separating church and state and ensuring that no religious significance at all be attached to this season. Make sure it all relates to Spring and natures natural emergence.

We have kicked the Enemy out of the public schools but we need to do a better job of getting him booted out of government and all public life. Remember our goal is to get the Enemy out of government and then to grow government to take over all of life in the U.S. A huge secular government controlling most of life in America is our formula for taking America down. We're nearly there. The day when people look to Gov't not God for their needs and rights isn't far away - many already do.

I can't tell you how pleased we were when President Obama went to Turkey and announced that the U.S.A. was not a Christian nation. He followed that by three times leaving the word "Creator" out of the Declaration of Independence when reciting it. This was followed by Senator Harry Reid leaving "Under God" out of his reciting of the Pledge of Allegiance. Keep up this great work! The Democrats and the Ruling Class are embarrassed by America's Christian heritage use that to get them to deny it or omit it in public whenever they have a chance. Don't let up a bit we have America on the ropes! Be sure you keep the Democrat Party moving farther away from any vestiges of Christianity.

Your Brilliant and Humble Professor

X

Luscious Academianut Ph.D.

LETTERS FROM PERVERSE UNIVERSITY

Following is one of a series of letters intercepted by Dr. L. James Harvey. They are from a Professor of Deception at Perverse University in Hell and are sent to his former students who are in the U.S.A. working to tempt America away from its Judeo/Christian values. Dr. Harvey has edited the profanity out of the letters and presents them for your information.

Perverse University ™

Department of Deception
P.O. Box 666
Smoke City, Hades 66666

Home of the Fighting Red Devils

The Solomon Solution

Dear Sextwister,

I have to say we are delighted with the success you have had in compromising, weakening, and sucking the spiritual vitality out of the major protestant denominations in the U.S. We were thrilled when the Presbyterian Church U.S.A. approved the ordination of homosexuals. They are now split, divided, spiritually weakened, losing members, and pose no threat to us whatsoever. Since the sexual revolution of the 1960s in the U.S. we have been able, largely through your good work, to take down the U.C.C., the Episcopal Church, the ELCA, the Presbyterians U.S.A., and we'll soon have the UMC. Fantastic! All of these denominations are badly split and dying and all because you used the Solomon Solution and the homosexual issue to compromise their integrity.

We are so proud of your work we have developed a case study for use here at P.U. to help educate our students on how to turn the Enemy's own character against him. When our Father Satan devised the strategy and used it so effectively to bring down one of the Enemy's favorite patients and the wisest man who ever lived, we knew we had a winning strategy. As you so well know, our Father used Solomon's love and compassion for his pagan wives (he had 700 of them) to justify his building temples to their foreign gods in Israel. Idol worship grew out of compassion and some Israelites began worshiping idols. Wonderful! Our Father turned love and compassion (I hate to even use these disgusting words) to our purposes by getting Solomon to sin and to justify defying the Enemy. How sweet it was, and you have now gotten clergy and church leaders in the major denominations to use love and compassion for homosexuals to defy the Enemy's teachings, undermining his horrid book, and opening the door for all kinds of false beliefs. Defeating the Enemy by using love is a delicious victory for us whenever we can us it. Long live the Solomon Solution! Evil, justified by good, is a winner every time.

Now, you still have a lot of work to do so don't get complacent. Those pesky evangelicals are still fixated on the Enemy's horrid book. We must erode the commitments of the SBC, the Pentecostals, the Assembly of God folks, the IFCA Bible churches, and others who still cling to the inerrancy of that horrid book. As the secular society in the U.S. grows in its acceptance of sodomy you can use the Solomon Solution on some of these groups. Encourage our gay friends to continue to call those opposed to them bigots and homophobes, and use those wonderful nondiscrimination laws that include sexual orientation to prosecute anyone, including pastors who speak negatively about sodomy or gay marriage. These and other sexual sins will bring the U.S. down before long. Look how we've undermined the Catholic Church through homosexuality and pedophilia. We're winning! Keep up the good fight.

Your Magnificent and Wise mentor,

X

Luscious Academianut Ph.D.

LETTERS FROM PERVERSE UNIVERSITY

Following is one of a series of letters intercepted by Dr. L. James Harvey. They are from a Professor of Deception at Perverse University in Hell and are sent to his former students who are in the U.S.A. working to tempt America away from its Judeo/Christian values. Dr. Harvey has edited the profanity out of the letters and presents them for your information.

Perverse University ™

Department of Deception
P.O. Box 666
Smoke City, Hades 66666

Home of the Fighting Red Devils

Temptation 101

Dear Enticer,

We have recently received some interesting data regarding the American public and their greatest temptations. This, of course, tracks the success you are having in leading Americans astray. This is in essence your score card and we must say you are doing very well particularly among the younger Americans where our battle for evil is most important, and fortunately for you, where you are having the greatest success.

The data, collected by the Barna Group, tracks info on the four major generational groups roughly as follows: Millennials ages 18 to 29, Busters ages 30 to 45, Boomers ages 46 to 65, and Elders 66 +

The major temptations that are fairly common to all groups are as follows with the percentages reported by all study participants:

Procrastination – 60%
Worrying – 60%
Eating too much (gluttony) – 55%
Spending too much time on the media – 44%
Spending too much money - 44%
Being lazy and not working as hard as I should (slothfulness) – 41%

You are doing well on these, particularly the gluttony and slothfulness the Enemy warns his people about, but you can do better on some of the others. Gossiping 26%, Feeling jealous 24% and viewing pornography 18% should be much higher.

The good news regarding pornography is that the Millennials are the largest group mentioning this as a temptation at 27% while only 8% of the Elders do. It's also great to see that women are viewing pornography as much as men are. If we can reasonably assume that some survey respondents are not fully truthful about viewing pornography, we can assume this figure is much higher for the younger people. Combined with the data we are getting about younger people in high school and college regularly "hooking up," we are well on the way to destroying the chances for the younger generation to ever establish the strong traditional family that most often teach their children those values of the Enemy we hate so much. Pornography and promiscuity lead to broken marriages, no fault divorces, and that wonderful growing statistic we now see that in the U.S. that 40% of all children will never live with both natural parents. As we taught you here at old P.U., we can destroy Christian America with broken families and children who are undisciplined, hedonistic, and have contempt for their elders. We are seeing the beginning of the results of your efforts in the "flash mobs" and teenage gangs that are terrorizing many cities in the U.S. and the new "Knockout" phenomena that is sweeping America. Chaos through mob violence is so delicious. Keep up the good work.

Your Dazzling and Spectacular Professor,

X

Luscious Academianut Ph.D.

🔥 LETTERS FROM PERVERSE UNIVERSITY 🔥

Following is one of a series of letters intercepted by Dr. L. James Harvey. They are from a Professor of Deception at Perverse University in Hell and are sent to his former students who are in the U.S.A. working to tempt America away from its Judeo/Christian values. Dr. Harvey has edited the profanity out of the letters and presents them for your information.

Perverse University ™

Department of Deception
P.O. Box 666
Smoke City, Hades 66666

Home of the Fighting Red Devils

The "Iron Triangle" Works!

Dear Debtlover,

Our Father Satan is ecstatic over how well the "Iron Triangle" is working in the U.S. We are beside ourselves down here, as we see how our Father Satan's well-designed strategy has brought America and some of America's greatest political entities to the brink of bankruptcy. It took longer than we had hoped, but now we will increasingly reap the fruits of your good work. The U.S. and some cities and political sub-divisions will soon go bankrupt. Public service unions, Democrat voters, and Democrat elected officials, is the beautiful "Iron Triangle." The Democrat officials' voters elect negotiate sweetheart contracts they can't afford for Democrat teachers and public officials with borrowed money, and pass the debt to future generations. That's our Father's "Iron Triangle" and prescription for destroying America. Adding some delicious corruption by elected officials and union leaders along the way is just frosting on the cake. The extravagant salaries and promised pensions are now coming home to roost as our Father predicted.

We taught you well here in Deception 101. Our Father's strategy to get American public service workers unionized, in spite of the warning against this by President Franklin D. Roosevelt, was genius. The plan works because the public officials, who sign the sweetheart contracts are averse to raising taxes to pay for the promises they make so they pass the costs of the contracts on to future generations by borrowing money, which in turn increases their spending to fund the interest on the borrowed money. Our Father Satan was right to assume these incestuous relations or iron triangles would eventually bankrupt American cities, counties, and states. Detroit, that iconic American city, in 2014 led other American political sub-divisions into that glorious bankruptcy which, if we play it right, will lead to demonstrations and riots as public service employees find the benefits promised them are being taken away. Marvelous chaos can soon develop across America.

The beauty of this is that the unions will ask the Democrat presidents and Senates they elected to bail them out by giving them the money to pay for their benefits. This recently happened, as you know when Biden and the Democrats passed their so-called infrastructure bill which bailed out Illinois and some large cities at least temporarily. The glorious truth is the government is already bankrupt because of their own "Iron Triangle" made up of government workers, unions, and welfare recipients who elect Democrats who have given them benefits beyond reality and passed the bill on to future generations by borrowing trillions of dollars they can never repay. When the rest of the world realizes that America has been diluting the value of the dollar by printing paper with no supporting value the dollar, as a worldwide reserve currency, will collapse and the American economy will be thrown into a glorious depression. Riots and chaos will follow and the American society will finally reap the rewards our Father Satan has awaiting them.

Make sure any Americans who oppose our Father's plan continue to be labeled homophobes, bigots, feeble minded, and outdated. Make sure those "Make America Great Again" (MAGA) people continue to be neutralized by our good friends in the mainstream media and the IRS. You've done marvelous work. We have America on the brink – let's push them over the cliff.

Your Extraordinarily Gifted Professor,

X

Luscious Academianut Ph.D.

LETTERS FROM PERVERSE UNIVERSITY

Following is one of a series of letters intercepted by Dr. L. James Harvey. They are from a Professor of Deception at Perverse University in Hell and are sent to his former students who are in the U.S.A. working to tempt America away from its Judeo/Christian values. Dr. Harvey has edited the profanity out of the letters and presents them for your information.

Perverse University ™

Department of Deception
P.O. Box 666
Smoke City, Hades 66666

Home of the Fighting Red Devils

Use the White Robes!

Dear Subterfuge,

I can't tell you how happy we are down here to see your victory in the U.S. Supreme Court on gay marriage. The Obergefell v. Hodges case made gay marriage legal and it made sodomy a right of all Americans. The strategy we taught you down here of dressing evil in the white robes of goodness is working wonderfully well. The sin of sodomy and sexual immorality has been wonderfully dressed up as love and rights while those opposing gay rights have been cloaked in the black robes of bigotry and homophobia. Fantastic! Getting people to do evil for a good reason is one of our Father Satan's greatest inventions. This trick has even confused some of the Enemy's own people into helping our cause. Justice Anthony Kennedy a conservative voted with the four liberal justices to give the homosexuals a 5-4 decision on a matter that the Constitution indicates, because of the 10 Amendment, SCOTUS had no right to decide. Kennedy was won over because of the "White Robes." Wonderful!

Our father Satan couldn't be prouder of you for using the strategy he perfected in the Garden of Eden where he convinced Eve that eating the forbidden fruit was actually a good thing for her. He dressed the sin in a white robe and she fell for it. Even though the Enemy warned his people in his horrid book that Father Satan was the father of lies and would be disguised as an angel of light and would blind the eyes of the unbelievers, and you his servants would also masquerade as servants of righteousness (read also white robes). (II Corinthians 11:14-15) We're still winning.

Now in America you have done very well with this strategy. You've dressed killing unborn children up in the white robe of women's rights. You've blanked the U.S. with casinos and lotteries under the white robe of raising money to improve the education of children and now you are winning some wonderful victories for the use of marijuana under the white robe of medical necessity to combat pain. You must now dress some of our other sexual sins in the white robe of love and rights. The Americans are suckers for that one and you should be able to get them to accept polygamy, bestiality, pedophilia, and incest dressed in the same white gowns of love and rights you used for sodomy. We've got America on the bus to Gomorrah don't let them get off.

We just finished drinking a toast to Associate Justice Anthony Kennedy whose vote determined the gay marriage case. Justice Kennedy (get this) while wearing a black robe was hoodwinked by the white robe, we threw over sodomy and homosexuality and ruled in our favor. Kennedy also authored the Lawrence v. Texas opinion which made sodomy a right in Texas some years ago and opened the door for gay rights. His former clerk says Kennedy is truly the Supreme Courts first gay judge and all while wearing a beautiful black robe the favorite color of our Father Satan. It can't get much better for us. Keep up the good work and use more white robes to hide our true color.

Your Brilliant, Handsome, and Gay Professor,

X

Luscious Academianut Ph.D.

LETTERS FROM PERVERSE UNIVERSITY

Following is one of a series of letters intercepted by Dr. L. James Harvey. They are from a Professor of Deception at Perverse University in Hell and are sent to his former students who are in the U.S.A. working to tempt America away from its Judeo/Christian values. Dr. Harvey has edited the profanity out of the letters and presents them for your information.

Perverse University ™

Department of Deception
P.O. Box 666
Smoke City, Hades 66666

Home of the Fighting Red Devils

Societal Suicide

Dear Nationkiller,

In our course Nation Destruction 201 we are now using a new textbook. I'm enclosing a copy and I want you and all your staff to read and study it. It describes in detail how our Father Satan has brought down societies over the last 4500 years. The book entitled, **"The Collapse of Complex Societies"** by Joseph Tainter describes how 27 separate complex civilizations over history have literally destroyed themselves through greed, bureaucratic profligacy, and corruption. They all literally committed suicide. You will be thrilled to read that we have the U.S.A. going down the exact same path that led each of these civilizations to their ultimate demise. This book gives you a further template to follow as you work to facilitate the suicide of the U.S.A.

As you study Tainter, you will find two basic trends that sealed the fate of the 27 societies. The first was the development of a wealthy upper class that drained productive resources from the society for profligate living creating a monumental income gap between themselves and the rest of their society. They drained the financial life blood out of their people and used it for decadent living. The second factor that brought these societies down was the unstoppable growth of their bureaucratic governments which also drained productive resources from society creating a bureaucracy with an unquenchable thirst for money to pay for growth. These two forces together ultimately led these governments into debasing their currencies to pay bills and ultimate bankruptcy when all alternatives to obtaining further resources ran out. Chaos inevitably ensued leading to a collapse of the civilization. My letter next month will deal with how we can best use the government and bureaucratic beast to drain the life blood out of the country.

In America today we have both factors Tainter mentioned working nicely. The government bureaucracy is growing by leaps and bounds. Obamacare added thousands of new bureaucrats and further drained productive capital from society. The wealth gap is also becoming wider as the rich at the top (Bankers, corporate and hedge fund executives, sports figures, entertainers, etc.) make obscene salaries and profits while those at the bottom of society live on food stamps and government handouts inviting them to become lazy and unproductive. It couldn't be better for us. The U.S. is debasing its currency inviting a debilitating inflation and threatening the dollars status as the world's reserve currency. It is not out of the question that we could see some delicious riots and chaos in America as the lower classes become aware of how their corrupt government, aided and abetted by the wealthy, has sold them out for their own personal benefits. Isn't greed simply delicious?

Continue the culture war on Christianity. We must drive all vestiges of it out of public life in the U.S. Christians and the Enemy with their hated values are the only ones that can undermine our success. Step up efforts by the gays, the ACLU, the atheists, the radical feminists, and those wonderful liberal lukewarm Christians, who have been so helpful in the past. Continue to paint serious Christians as outdated, bigoted, homophobes, who cling to their guns and Bibles in times of trouble. Make sure Americans continue to believe they are invincible and what happened to earlier civilizations couldn't possibly happen to them. Hide the truth from them that the earth is littered with the ruins of nations who believed they were everlasting. We have them on the run! Press on at all costs!

Your Brilliant and Precocious Professor,
X
Luscious Academianut Ph.D.

Following is one of a series of letters intercepted by Dr. L. James Harvey. They are from a Professor of Deception at Perverse University in Hell and are sent to his former students who are in the U.S.A. working to tempt America away from its Judeo/Christian values. Dr. Harvey has edited the profanity out of the letters and presents them for your information.

Perverse University ™

Department of Deception
P.O. Box 666
Smoke City, Hades 66666

Home of the Fighting Red Devils

Hi-Tech Immorality

Dear Sexup,

We're thrilled at the reports we are getting down here about how you and your colleagues have enticed the Americans to use new hi-tech devices to increase their immoral conduct. The new cell phones and apps that hook-up sexual encounters are simply wonderful. From middle school kids to senior citizens looking for a sexual encounter the hi-tech devices make it ultra-easy to find a willing partner willing to commit adultery.

We were delighted to see the scope and magnitude of the publicized web site Ashley Madison developed which promoted adultery among married people. While the publicity hurt us temporally the word spread and is giving rise to other similar web sites spreading the immorality further. The cell phone apps which easily link those looking for sexual encounters are helping our cause in a marvelous way. High school and college kids can get on their phones and find a hook-up within minutes when they feel the desire to find some sexual pleasure. This is making some college campuses virtual bordellos on the weekends. The fact that most public colleges no longer believe they have any responsibility for the sexual conduct of students (remember we long ago got rid of that horrid "en loco parentis" concept) has allowed healthy red blooded young students to let their libidos run wild. The fact that colleges no longer teach values and de facto model secular humanism, which glorifies self and self-gratification, makes our job that much easier.

We are now reaping the rewards of your good efforts in increased STDs, unwanted pregnancies and abortions, and sexual conduct making traditions marriages almost impossible. Fantastic! We have also received information that HIV/Aids is making a wonderful comeback after diminishing for a time. Many young gays no longer believe AIDs is a fatal disease, and that even if they get it, new drugs will save them, so they seldom use protection. Well over 1.2 million Americans are now living with Aids and more die each year than are killed on the highways through drunk driving accidents. 90% of Aids transmission is through sexual conduct, most between gay men. There's even another blessing here for us because when a gay man gets Aids, he goes on a drug cocktail which costs over $60,000 a year. Since most can't afford that they go on welfare and the bankrupt U.S. government must pick up the tab for the rest of their life. Do you see the beauty in that for us? It's a wonderful doubleheader: we ruin a life and help drive the U.S. even further into bankruptcy.

Keep the sexual destruction going. Make sure more and more pornography is available over the internet so even children can view it with their cell phones any time they wish. Make swinging and hooking-up so easy and cheap that more and more Americans of all ages will be tempted to seek sexual gratification on a daily basis. Sodom and Gomorrah and the days of Noah will engulf America and the Enemy will be embarrassed to tears.

Make every new hi-tech device that comes along an instrument for increasing the sexual destruction of the U.S.A. Father Satan is excited about your work and the wonderful progress you're making.

Your Wonderful and Brilliant Professor,

X

Luscious Academianut Ph.D.

Following is one of a series of letters intercepted by Dr. L. James Harvey. They are from a Professor of Deception at Perverse University in Hell and are sent to his former students who are in the U.S.A. working to tempt America away from its Judeo/Christian values. Dr. Harvey has edited the profanity out of the letters and presents them for your information.

Perverse University ™

Department of Deception
P.O. Box 666
Smoke City, Hades 66666

Home of the Fighting Red Devils

The Flower Lady

Dear Courtdown,

We think we just won a major court victory, but we aren't totally sure. We just heard that the Flower Lady Barronelle Stutzman in the State of Washington sold her flower shop and went out of business ending close to a decade of your persecution of her for refusing to do a flower arrangement for a homosexual customer's wedding. The case, as you'll recall went all the way to the Supreme Court (SCOTUS). They sent the case back to the Supreme Court of the State of Washington that had originally ruled against Barronelle. We thought we had lost down here when that happened, but the Washington court ruled against her a second time and then SCOTUS did us a huge favor and refused to hear a second appeal leaving the final decision in the Washington court and against the Flower Lady. Thank Satan SCOTUS failed to follow through with the preservation of religious freedom we thought they had determined. The ruling gives us great hope for future SCOTUS rulings.

I think we've won, however, while Stutzman has been put out of business the Enemy's folks are treating her like a hero for fighting us for nearly 10 years and they are encouraging others to bring similar cases. In fact, there is another case right now from Colorado 303 Creative v. Elenis which is being appealed to SCOTUS and could hurt us badly, if they rule incorrectly. As you know, in this case a Christian web designer, Lorrie Smith, refused to design a web site which celebrated same sex weddings. As you'll remember, Colorado is particularly hostile to Christians who want to enjoy the freedom to live by their religious beliefs as demonstrated by their support of our values in the Cake Case discussed earlier. If SCOTUS is consistent, we may still be dealt a serious blow if they rule against us. Be sure you marshal all the resources including our LGBTQ friends who have a lot invested in the outcome of this case. Get as many organizations as you can find to file amicus briefs supporting the Colorado Civil Rights Commission whose ruling against the 303 Creative software company is being appealed.

There is one more thing you must give 100% of your effort too. This Christian legal firm that represented the Flower Lady and is representing 303 Creative is a pain to us. They've represented others against us as well and you must do everything possible to hurt and destroy them if possible. This firm, Alliance Defending Freedom (ADF) is representing Christians we're attacking and they are doing it for free! They raise money from Christians all over the country and then train Christian attorneys from all over the country to support Christians usually pro bono when legal issues particularly regarding freedom of religion issues come up. See if you can get some dirty material on one or more of their key attorneys. Find something illegal, disbar them if you can and see if you can stop the flow of money to the organization. They are a pain and Father Satan goes into a rage every time that organization is mentioned. There are some other similar legal organizations that have sprung up but the ADF is causing us the most problems right now and they are winning far more than they should. Kill them!

Your Magnificent and Supremely Talented Professor,

X

Luscious Academianut Ph.D.

Following is one of a series of letters intercepted by Dr. L. James Harvey. They are from a Professor of Deception at Perverse University in Hell and are sent to his former students who are in the U.S.A. working to tempt America away from its Judeo/Christian values. Dr. Harvey has edited the profanity out of the letters and presents them for your information.

Perverse University ™

Department of Deception
P.O. Box 666
Smoke City, Hades 66666

Home of the Fighting Red Devils

The Debt Killer

Dear Dollardown,

Father Satan is delighted with the progress you've achieved in destroying the American economy. He was in the faculty lounge the other day and he listed some of your achievements. He was particularly proud of the following:

1. It's been 67 years since the U.S. reduced its national debt. The last time the debt at the end of a fiscal year was lower than at the beginning was 1957 when Eisenhower was president. The debt is now 30 trillion and growing.

2. Barack Obama when a senator gave a speech where he emotionally castigated the republicans for increasing the national debt saying it was immoral to pass on debt to children and grandchildren with deficit spending. Yet when he became president Obama, in his 8 years, he ran up more national debt that all the previous presidents combined. What glorious hypocrisy. Obama continues to guide Biden through Susan Rice one of Obama's closest advisors, who has an office in the White House.

3. The U.S. debt to gross domestic product (GDP) is now 125% and rising. Any country which approaches 100% is in deep financial trouble.

4. The U.S. is spending about 6.8 trillion dollars a year in the federal budget and taking in about 3.8 trillion in taxes and revenue leaving projected annual budget deficits in the 3 trillion-dollar range. There is no serious effort to balance the budget or pay down on the structural debt in the foreseeable future guaranteeing a financial disaster. The dollar will collapse and be replaced by some other financial instrument as the world's reserve currency further destroying the American economy. Just what we want. Our friends in China and Russian are already working to make this happen. They are licking their chops.

5. The U.S. has the worst inflation in 40 years and its rising. Biden is proposing more taxes which will damage the economy further.

6. The U.S. is no longer energy independent; it now depends on OPEC. How wonderful!

7. The democrats are working hard to pass 5-6 trillion in more spending in upcoming years. They say it's paid for but we know it's one of our most wonderful lies. If the legislation passes, not only will it bankrupt America but the social legislation included will forever destroy America and create a socialist/communist nation that will be just like we want. America will be another success for us as has been Venezuela, China, Cuba, Zimbabwe, Nicaragua, and a host of others. We'll be on our way to our one world government.

8. Two million illegal immigrants will pour into the U.S. this year changing the nations character. Biden will give them free healthcare, food stamps and education. They will eventually vote for our Democrat friends turning the U.S. socialist, and keeping it so.

9. We were delighted to see Biden commit one of the nation's worst foreign policy blunders when leaving Afghanistan. He left American citizens behind and 85 billion dollars in the latest military equipment. He made America the joke of the world and projected a weakness that

now invites China to threaten Taiwan. Biden is doing great things for us. Keep him in office!

Here are the things Father Satan said could hurt us. Work on these!

1. A book has come out entitled, "Lap Top from Hell," it proves Joe Biden and his family, particularly Hunter, are corrupt. Joe may be impeached over it if Republicans ever win the House but that won't hurt us much because Kamala will be as good for us as Joe.

2. Make sure the Democrats get a bill or two through to increase spending beyond the structural debt mentioned in #4 above. If they can't get 5-6 trillion more let them compromise to 3-4 if it can get some more debt added. We need more debt. Pile it on!

3. Kill the attempts that idiot Mike Lindell is still working on to over throw the 2020 election. Lindell is trying to get several key states, where there is provable voter fraud in the 2020 election, to recall their electors' votes and take a case to the Supreme Court to have the election overturned. The Supreme Court, if they take the case, could then either declare Trump the winner and install him as president, or they could throw the election to the House of Representatives, which would elect Trump (because each state has one vote on the matter), or they could order revotes in critical states. **We can't let that happen!** Get rid of Lindell! He's already got several states to agree and audits are underway in Wisconsin, Pennsylvania, Georgia, and possibly Michigan. The Arizona audit proved there were over 80,000 questionable votes in a state Trump only lost by 10,000. Further investigation could turn Arizona to Trump. Worst of all a new study indicates 35% of Americans believe the 2020 election was stolen. We can't let that percentage grow. **Give stopping all this top priority.** If this isn't stopped, you will be recalled and punished severely, according to what Father Satan said.

Your Brilliant and Insightful Professor,

X

Luscious Academianut Ph.D.

LETTERS FROM PERVERSE UNIVERSITY

Following is one of a series of letters intercepted by Dr. L. James Harvey. They are from a Professor of Deception at Perverse University in Hell and are sent to his former students who are in the U.S.A. working to tempt America away from its Judeo/Christian values. Dr. Harvey has edited the profanity out of the letters and presents them for your information.

Perverse University ™

Department of Deception
P.O. Box 666
Smoke City, Hades 66666

Home of the Fighting Red Devils

World View

Dear Chief of Deceptors,

Father Satan was reviewing our master strategy for taking over countries in preparation for creating the one world government which Father Satan will one day rule. Our strategies for taking over individual countries have had successes, but has not always succeeded as we'd hoped. We won Germany and Russia, and then lost them both. We're winning back Russia though with our friend Putin. We won Cuba, Zimbabwe, Venezuela, Nicaragua, China, and some others but the big prize we must take down is the U.S.A.

We are making good progress, but there is growing opposition we must neutralize. We won the big 2020 election through fraud and we must capitalize on it before our opposition can recover. We have won the education system in the U.S. from the Ivy league down through the elementary schools with our Critical Race Theory (CRT) and 1619 Project, plus our wonderful socialist lie that if people would only let us rule the nation we would bring peace, prosperity, and our marvelous equity to everyone. We've also gained control of the military by buying off the Joint Chiefs and the Secretary of Defense and the Defense Department. It looks like we also have control of the Department of Justice, CIA, and FBI. We must now get that legislation passed in Congress to give us control of all future elections to insure we retain control of the government. Biden is helping by getting many justices confirmed who share our views, but we need to expand the Supreme Court to insure our final victory. Work hard to help Biden pack the Supreme Court.

Our friend George Soros has helped a great deal by funding the elections of numerous prosecuting attorneys and district attorneys in large Democrat cities. They are releasing criminals, failing to prosecute crimes, and removing bail requirements. This is leading to a rapid rise in crime and creating the kind of chaos in cities that we thrive on by promising those citizens, if they would just give us full control, we would solve all their problems and bring economic equity to all as well. Our cancel culture movement is kind of stalled. We need more statues taken down and more attempts to destroy the Declaration of Independence and Constitution, particularly the First Amendment promising freedom of religion and speech. Keep empathizing that these documents were developed by white slave owners to ensure slavery would be forever protected.

Our control of the public education system must indoctrinate this in all students.

Now, the Enemy's people are planning a major attack to undue all our good work. They are trying to reform the election laws in the states, which is why we must pass the legislation giving that function to the Federal government so we can get rid of photo IDs and preserve unlimited absentee voting to preserve our victory from 2020. The Enemy's people are also praying for a great awakening and revival, which if it happens will set us back immeasurably. Do everything you can to kill this effort. Use our gay friends, who have gained major footholds in some of the large denominations and mega churches to oppose a revival because it would be a threat to their gains, if there was a revival among strong Bible believing Christians.

You must also work harder to get the FBI to threaten parents with arrest if they are too vociferous in their attempts to kill CRT. Use our friends in the major teachers' unions to help us on this. They are all supportive of the liberal Democrat socialists so they should insist that they know better how and what to teach children that their parents do.

Keep up the good fight. We've got the U.S.A. on the ropes. Don't let them off. This victory would be our biggest and greatest yet.

Your Adorable and Brilliant Professor,

X

Luscious Academianut Ph.D.

P.S. #1—We just heard that justice Breyer has resigned and our friend Biden has promised to appoint a black woman, which violates the anti-discrimination law and the Constitution. Wonderful! Help him to appoint a dedicated black woman who supports CRT, abortion, gay rights, and open borders. We have control of all the agencies that could possibly prosecute him. They haven't prosecuted Hunter Biden, Hillary Clinton, Antifa, or Black Lives Matter. We've won. They won't prosecute Papa Joe Biden either.

P.S. #2—I can't tell you how proud we are of your Diversity Equity and Inclusion (DEI) programs. Organizations of all types are hiring Diversity Directors and running assessments and programs to educate everyone on white racism. The University of Southern Illinois is even starting a new Ph.D. program in DEI. We'll have the U.S.A. saturated with CRT and DEI before long.

Following is one of a series of letters intercepted by Dr. L. James Harvey. They are from a Professor of Deception at Perverse University in Hell and are sent to his former students who are in the U.S.A. working to tempt America away from its Judeo/Christian values. Dr. Harvey has edited the profanity out of the letters and presents them for your information.

Perverse University ™

Department of Deception
P.O. Box 666
Smoke City, Hades 66666

Home of the Fighting Red Devils

Kill the Best

Dear Generationdown,

We are thrilled by the latest data from the U.S.A. on your efforts to kill off the most productive Americans. Americans between 18 and 49 tend to be the most active and informed age group contributing to the progress of the country. They provide the heart and core of American energy, creativity, and progress and since the life expectancy in the U.S. is in the mid-70s they don't die very often, but because of covid-19 and your marvelous efforts to addict this group with drug addiction, they are dying in increasing numbers. Recent data show that deaths in this age group in 2021 was up annually more than 40%. More than 90,000 more deaths were reported in that age group with the largest contributor to the deaths being drug overdoses not covid-19. The increasing addition of the drug fentanyl to the drugs Americans use is doing the trick. Fentanyl, as you know, is 100 times more potent than morphine, and 50 times more potent than heroin. One pill can often kill. That's a winner for us. Keep up the great work.

We can't tell you how excited we are that, after the U.S. started blocking the importation of fentanyl directly into the U.S. from China, you found a way to have the Chinese Communist Party (CCP), which has been pushing these efforts, find a way of getting the drugs into the U.S. through

Mexico. It was brilliant to get the CCP to develop agreements with some Mexican criminal cartels. Now the CCP ships the precursors to fentanyl to the cartels which process them into the drug and then, thanks to President Biden, ship them into the U.S. through the wide-open border with the U.S. This drug traffic will only grow more and the American deaths in their most productive age group can easily double in the near future. This can irreparably damage the U.S. economy and nation. The former acting commissioner of Customs and Border Protection, Mark Morgan, recently said about the border, "This is not a surge. This is an invasion, I mean, a catastrophic number of illegal aliens trying to break into our country." Some estimate as many as 2 million will have entered in Biden's first year in office along with uncountable amounts of drugs. We can only dream of the destruction that will be visited upon America if our friend Biden stays president for a full 4 years. Father Satan is ecstatic about the progress you've made in this area. I think he may be considering giving you one of P.U.'s highest awards.

We have been impressed that within a relatively short time this new drug fentanyl, which is a synthetic opioid, has become so popular and lethal. And the joint efforts with the Mexican drug cartels was brilliant. We can destroy the U.S. within a short period of time. Our efforts are, of course, aided by the Biden's payments to American workers to stay home and not go to work because of covid-19. Reports are that there are now close to 10 million unfilled jobs in the U.S. If we continue to kill hundreds of thousands of their most productive workers, we can only dream of the damage that will be done to America. They will be destroyed.

Now, you must be vigilant the Enemy's people are praying for a great awakening. If that happens the American appetite for drugs could evaporate and hurt our efforts. Also, the Republicans are plotting to take over Congress later this year and the White House as soon as possible, if this happens the southern border will be closed, the wall completed, and the importation of drugs across the border stopped. Resist these efforts with all your might. We can't let them happen!

Keep up the great work. You are one of our most productive soldiers and I am proud to say one of my most brilliant former students.

Your Exquisitely Dazzling Superb Professor,

X

Luscious Academianut Ph.D.

LETTERS FROM PERVERSE UNIVERSITY

Following is one of a series of letters intercepted by Dr. L. James Harvey. They are from a Professor of Deception at Perverse University in Hell and are sent to his former students who are in the U.S.A. working to tempt America away from its Judeo/Christian values. Dr. Harvey has edited the profanity out of the letters and presents them for your information.

Perverse University ™

Department of Deception
P.O. Box 666
Smoke City, Hades 66666

Home of the Fighting Red Devils

Open Borders

Dear Nationdown,

We can't tell you how pleased we are that the Biden administration continues to violate American immigration law by the de facto opening of the Southern border of the U.S. It is estimated that approximately 2 million illegal immigrants have entered the U.S. during the first year of Biden's administration due to his failure to allow the American border and immigration services to carry out the law, as was the case under previous presidents.

You need to be careful, however, these late-night flights and bus rides which take the illegals all over the country and dump them in areas that have not been notified they are coming, is getting bad press. In fact, Governor DeSantis of Florida is taking legal and other actions against the government and private contractors involved to stop these drop offs of illegals. The American public is also becoming more and more concerned about the open border because the people coming in aren't vetted and its clear some criminals, covid-19 infected persons, and even some identified terrorists have been caught trying to get in. Most Americans now feel the horrible Biden border policy ranks right up there with the Afghanistan withdrawal as Biden's greatest presidential blunder to date.

Now in spite of the bad publicity, even if it costs the Democrats the presidential election of 2024, it could be worth it to us. Think how great it would be if over Biden's four years in office we could get 8 million illegal immigrants into the country. These people will all be Democrat voters legally or illegally. Bless New York City which just approved illegals voting in their city elections. Get more Democrat cities to do this plus push hard for amnesty for all illegals. If we can get this done the Republicans will never win a national election ever again.

Father Satan is not forgetting, by the way, that the open border is serving some other needs we have that are even more harmful to the U.S. The drugs, particularly fentanyl is killing off some of the most energetic and talented Americans in the 20-45 age group. In addition, the drug cartels are making millions off the child sex traffic and the forcing of illegal immigrant women into prostitution to pay off the debt incurred in bring them into the country. A border that Trump had largely closed is now wide open. Even the wall that Trump had close to finishing has been stopped at a cost of over a billion in lost dollars due to Biden's actions. Biden has totally surrendered to the Chamber of Commerce and the large businesses that want the cheap labor illegal immigrants bring into the country. This whole scenario is playing right into our hands do everything you can to keep the border open and the flow of drugs and illegals coming in increasing numbers. Watch out, however, if the Republicans take back the House and/or the Senate in the 2022 Fall elections they could start some investigations and prosecutions that could set us back. Do not let that happen!

Your Brilliant and Talented Professor,

X

Luscious Academianut Ph.D.

Perverse University ™

Department of Deception
P.O. Box 666
Smoke City, Hades 66666

Home of the Fighting Red Devils

Laziness

Dear Characterdown,

Father Satan wanted me to pass along to all our soldiers in the U.S.A. that overriding truth that laziness has been one of the best tools we have used down through the centuries to take down major empires. He wanted me to remind you that this characteristic was one that infected the critical leaders of nearly every major empire we took down including Rome, Greece, and Egypt and its one we need to encourage even more in the U.S.A.

He wanted to remind you that the pattern we have followed in all our wonderful historical successes was to have the leadership class in the great empires to become so successful and wealthy that they became addicted to wealth, power, immorality, sex, and soft living as their successes piled up. They began to hire other people to do the tough work they had done in building the empire. They started using more slaves to do their work and mercenaries to do their fighting. They began living what they called, the good life, and they and their children became addicted to living lives of focusing on pleasure and then debauchery as well. It only took a couple of generations living this way to create a weak corrupt hedonistic leadership class that helped these civilizations become weak, lazy, and ultimately to fall to younger vibrant societies who conquered them. Almost all great societies basically rotted from within and laziness was one of the characteristics of their demise.

Now the Enemy in his horrid book warns his people about laziness, but in so doing most translations use the word sloth which most Americans gloss right over. And few pastors have the courage to preach on the concept of laziness for fear of angering their parishioners. That's good for us. The Enemy warns about laziness (sloth) in numerous biblical passages including Proverbs 13:4, 12:24, 15:19, 21:25-26, and other places and in II Thessalonians 3:10 it was suggested that if a person didn't work, they shouldn't eat. Our soldiers need to do everything possible to promote laziness among Americans. Fortunately, President Biden and the Democrats have been helping a great deal since covid-19 hit paying Americans not to go to work and paying Americans for not working. They have given billions of dollars to teachers' unions in largely Democrat controlled cities to stay at home and the unions have worked to keep the schools closed harming the learning of students while teachers got paid to stay home. All this type of activity helps promote laziness and damages the nation's work ethic. Father Satan believes the top leadership in the U.S.A. is now showing signs of being soft, corrupt, wealthy, and hedonistic. One or two generations of this and the U.S.A. will be knocked off its perch as a world leading country. It won't ever again be a "shinning city on a hill" they'll be has-beens down in the dumps surpassed and superseded by a younger more energetic and progressive society perhaps China.

Keep our soldiers working hard. We've got the U.S.A. just about where we want them. Their future is dim if the Enemy's people don't have a mass awakening.

Your Glorious and Magnificent Professor,

X

Luscious Academianut Ph.D.

LETTERS FROM PERVERSE UNIVERSITY

Following is one of a series of letters intercepted by Dr. L. James Harvey. They are from a Professor of Deception at Perverse University in Hell and are sent to his former students who are in the U.S.A. working to tempt America away from its Judeo/Christian values. Dr. Harvey has edited the profanity out of the letters and presents them for your information.

Perverse University ™

Department of Deception
P.O. Box 666
Smoke City, Hades 66666

Home of the Fighting Red Devils

Lecture on Roman Demise

Memo To: Soldiers in America
From: Dr. Luscious Academianut
Re: Roman Demise and American Successes

Father Satan gave a lecture last week to my deceptions classes that was outstanding and I want you all to know what he said. Father first listed all the reasons that the Roman Empire in the West collapsed in 476 AD. He then compared this wonderful success we had in taking Rome down to the successes we are having in the U.S.A. It gives a wonderful picture of how we are succeeding and a chance to see how close we are to victory. I have summarized Father Satan's comments below.

Father Satan began by listing the reasons for Rome's demise as agreed upon by most current scholars of the period and they were:

1. Corruption in the government and incompetent leadership. Between 235 and 285 AD Rome had 22 different Emperors most were corrupt and many were assassinated.

2. Economic distress – Massive debt, debased currency, corruption, and trade deficits led to chaos and rapidly increasing inflation.

3. Decline of Military – Lack of disciplined Roman soldiers led to use of conquered people to fill legion ranks and hiring of mercenaries to maintain order. This lowered morale, lowered discipline, and weakened the Roman army.

4. Low birth rate and destruction of the nuclear family led to fewer Roman citizens and an undisciplined youth and generation.

5. Destruction of religion – religious chaos (competing religions) led to moral chaos and a loss of a national discipline. Crimes of violence increased making most cities unsafe. Immorality spread throughout the empire. Greed and laziness became rampant.

Father Satan said some scholars list 8 -10 reasons for Rome's fall but these 5 are the most critical. Then Father Satan said look how we're doing on them in the U.S.A.

1. We have the most corrupt and incompetent president the U.S. has had in history. The federal government is populated by the "deep state" which worked to get rid of President Trump to preserve its own incompetence and corruption.

2. The national debt is out of control and approaching 30 trillion. The dollar is declining in value and the U.S. is facing an inflation that can destroy them economically. They continue a large trade deficit which feeds the problem.

3. The military is more concerned with Critical Race Theory, Diversity Equity and Inclusion, and white rage than in winning wars. The current military leadership is corrupted by politics and the quality of their military is being seriously eroded. Women, gays, and trans gendered are being actively recruited. Current military are being taught America has historically been dominated by white racists.

4. Americans have a declining birth rate and the left-wing Democrats oppose the nuclear family. They want the government to raise and control the children the way our friend Hitler did. They want to start indoctrinating them at 3 years of age in government childcare programs.

LETTERS FROM PERVERSE UNIVERSITY

5. The Christian faith is being eroded significantly. A recent study showed less than 10% of Christians hold a Christian world view. The main stream of Christians are self-centered and make a god of themselves rather than follow the Enemy and what his horrid book teaches. They are emersed in the prosperity gospel. Drug use is epidemic and personal pleasure rules the day even in the large mega churches. Greed, laziness, and gluttony are increasing.

Father Satan ended his comments by praising those of you working in the U.S. for your great work and felt our ultimate victory in America is only a matter of a short time. He said, "Keep up the great work" and I add my compliments as well.

L.A.

Postscript

If there is a battle going on between good and evil, questions arise such as; where is the battle being fought? What are the instruments used in the battle? Am I involved in the fight and in what way? When will the battle be over? Can I be certain I will be on the winning side? Fortunately for the Christian all these questions are answered in the Bible and we can know for certain how it all turns out.

Let's answer some of the last questions first. In the book of Revelations, we are told about the events of the end times. The Bible indicates that there will be a terrible final battle between the forces of good and evil at a place called Armageddon (Rev. 16:16). This final battle comes after a series of events described in various biblical prophesies in the books of Daniel and Revelations and other places. We are told that God's forces will be triumphant in this final battle and that Jesus will return as a victor. The battle will usher in a final judgement and defeat of evil ushering in an eternity with God for all believers. When the battle will take place no one but God himself knows (Matt. 24:36, Mark 13:32). Jesus says in John 14:3 that he is coming again and that he will take His followers to be with Him in paradise. The Bible also tells us in John 3:16 and John 4:16 that to be on the winning side we need to believe in and serve Jesus Christ. If we do that, then we can guarantee we will be on the winning side. If anyone reading this has not accepted Jesus Christ there is a sinners Prayer at the end of this postscript you can pray and if you're sincere in it you can be certain you will be saved and spend eternity with the winners in heaven.

But is there current conflict between good and evil and how is this confrontation carried out in the meantime? And are you and I involved in it? The answer is everyone is involved and the battle is basically being fought on a constant basis in the minds of each person. God and Satan are in a continuing struggle to win the souls and minds of every individual who lives. The battle takes place in the thoughts and ideas that pass through our minds and consciousness.

As was mentioned in the Introduction, the eminent Swiss psychiatrist, Paul Tournier believes God and Satan battle each other in our minds by placing thoughts and suggestions there which force us to make choices through the freedom of will God has given to each of us. In short, God and Satan constantly provide thoughts which we must contemplate and which force us to make decisions regarding our behavior. Our consciences help us make correct decisions, if we accept Christ into our lives, become sensitive to the leading of the Holy Spirit God sends to guide us, study His Holy Word, and seek to live a Christian life. However, Satan is always ready to tempt us to live lives of pleasure and materialism, in effect, tempting us to make a god of ourselves and making pleasure and success in this life our highest priority. The Bible tells us that the majority of people will surrender to Satan's "siren songs" and follow the broad pathway of self-centeredness and earthly pleasures to their ultimate demise, but we can follow the narrow pathway that leads to eternal life.

But let's step back for a minute. God in His wisdom chose to create us with a free will and the freedom to choose to love and serve Him or to reject Him and serve ourselves primarily. Self-centeredness is the default position for those who reject God. God gave us this choice because the only love that has any value to Him is one that is freely given. A forced love has no value. In fact, it is a non sequitur. The Bible also tells us that Satan is a fallen angel (Rev. 9) who, with his legions (fallen angels often referred to as demons) has been given power in this earth for a limited time to tempt people to serve him and reject God. And so, the battle then goes on in our minds. Both God and Satan have the power to present thoughts and influence our thinking and actions. We have the freedom to accept or reject thoughts, to entertain them or to reject them. Here are some principals that relate to this process.

Seldom if ever do single thoughts lead to sinful acts—Let's look at Judas Iscariot for example. We read in John 13:2 that the Devil "put into his heart" to betray Jesus. This means in modern terms (we know now that the mind not the heart is the center of thought) that Satan put into the mind of Judas the idea of betraying Jesus. Having received the idea Judas had the choice of keeping it and thinking about it or rejecting it. We have some indication from John 6:70-71 that Judas had a mind that would be receptive to the idea of betrayal because he was a "devil" already, meaning his mind contained thoughts and values which allowed a betrayal thought to be welcomed. Judas had not internalized the teachings of Jesus. He was a self-centered individual and an evil thought must have a fertile field in which to mature into an act, and Judas' mind was fertile soil for such a thought.

I must admit I have at times felt sorry for Judas Iscariot. It seemed almost unfair to me for him to have had just one evil thought, which he acted upon, and for which he then had so much sorrow that he went out and hung himself. A more careful look at the situation, however, indicates that Judas had an evil mind well before the betrayal and that he had numerous opportunities to accept the teachings of Jesus who he was serving, which would have canceled out the betrayal idea had the teachings of Jesus been internalized.

It is safe to say that just having an evil thought is never wrong in and of itself. In fact, it is a part of life to have both good and bad thoughts placed in our minds. The real question is what do we do with these thoughts. Do we dismiss the bad ones and ponder the good ones or vice versa?

Our thoughts are known by God and shape our being—The Bible says in many places (e.g. Genesis 6:5, Psalm 94:11, I Corinthians 3:20) that God knows our thoughts. Jesus knew people's thoughts when He was on earth (see Luke 6:6, Matthew 12:25). There is no place to escape God's knowledge of our thoughts. The Bible also states that our thoughts shape the essence of our being. Proverbs 23:7 indicates that "as a man thinketh so is he." These two truths ought to be sobering to Christians and teach us that harboring evil thoughts of any kind can shape our being and determine our actions (see Mark 7:21). A pure mind leads to peace, joy, and eternity.

An evil mind leads to sorrow, sin, judgment, and Hell. But God leaves the choice to us.

Evil thoughts can come from good people—there's an interesting example of this in Matthew 16-21-22. Jesus had just told his disciples that the chief priests and elders would kill him. Peter took Jesus aside and said that would never happen. Satan had planted an idea. Jesus then said to Peter, "get thee behind me Satan!" Jesus did not mean Peter was Satan. He meant that at that moment Peter was being used by Satan to present a thought to Him he knew to be wrong. In short, Christians are personally responsible for processing thoughts no matter where they come from and even good people can be used by Satan to tempt God's people. Even the church can be wrong, as it has been historically, teaching doctrines later proven to be contrary to God's truth (e.g., indulgences, segregation, and that the earth was flat and the center of the universe). In summary, we must always be conscious of our thoughts and whether they are consistent with God's word and will. Even thoughts coming from God's people and church must be tested. John Huss, Martin Luther, and other reformers did exactly that, and when they found the church of their day to be wrong, based on God's word, they correctly followed God's word. We can do no less.

God always provides a way out of temptation for his followers—No matter how strongly we are tempted God promises we will never be tempted beyond that which we can successfully resist. (I Corinthians 10:13). He also promised that with the temptation He will always provide a way out for us (I Corinthians 10:13). In short, the Christian has built in protection against being tempted if we just look for it. This promise of God, of course, makes it impossible for the Christian to scapegoat their shortcomings onto something or someone else. God does not abide excuses. A famous comedian, Flip Wilson, was known for frequently saying when caught in a bad circumstance that, "the devil made me do it." That's one excuse god will never accept. God simply replies that while Satan gave you the idea, I gave you the truth and a way out. You just failed to take it. You made a bad choice. It has been this way since Eve made the first wrong choice in the Garden of Eden and it will be to the end of time.

We can choose where we get most of our thoughts—We can choose who we associate with, what we read, what we want to see, and where we go. All of these choices help determine what kinds of thoughts we are likely to encounter. The mature Christian will spend time in God's word and will find the thoughts of God in other Christians, which will feed their thought processes. Associating with other Christians will feed positive thinking. As we mature in our faith, we also learn how to avoid the negative and sinful influences which can harm us and learn how Satan is likely to mount an attack on us if he wishes. I have to believe that as we grow in our faith Satan might lose interest in wasting time on us if we are strong believers. I doubt Satan wasted much time on Mother Teresa, when she was alive, or on Billy Graham during his life. Their minds were largely fixed on God and His will for their lives. I'm sure they also knew where the attacks of Satan would come from if he tried to compromise them and they erected proper defenses ahead of time. That's what Christians ought to do. In the book of James we read,

"If we resist the Devil, he will flee from us." If we choose to associate with those who tell dirty jokes, laugh at adultery, and make light of serious sins, we will have an inordinate number of evil thoughts sent our way with an increased level of temptations. If we choose to watch filthy shows on TV, use pornography, and go places where people are sinning, we put ourselves in unnecessary jeopardy. Our choices add up and determine our actions.

What can Christians do to Ensure Success in the Battle?

Here are some thoughts, which if followed, will help Christians develop a clean mind and a pure soul, thus avoiding much of the impact of the suggestions and temptations Satan inevitably sends our way.

A. **Read and study the Bible daily**—If we fill our minds with God's truths and teachings, we can more easily discern evil thoughts and drive out those that Satan invariably sends our way.

As one Christian said, "When we open the Bible God opens his mouth." God speaks to us through his word.

B. **Identify and listen to dedicated and mature Christians**—If serious mature Christians agree on an issue the chances are that it is God's will. Listen to some of the wonderful Christian pastors on the TV and radio. They will share God's word and will and may point you to the truth even on sensitive social and political issues that have a serious moral impact on our nation and society.

C. **Consciously avoid those who will temp you or lead you astray**—Unless you are actively seeking to convert a sinner, it is better to avoid those people who fill your mind with evil thoughts and ideas. Associating with God's people, literature, and media is the best way to put a wall between you and evil.

D. **Be conscious of the danger of entertaining evil thoughts**—Because our thoughts are private and hidden, we may assume if they aren't known they will be harmless. That's Satan's trump card. If we dwell on evil thoughts particularly if they give us some temporary pleasure, we are inviting difficulty. Remember that God knows our every thought. We can't hide them from Him.

We best get rid of them ASAP.

E. **Pray unceasingly to be kept from temptation**—The words of the prayer Jesus taught us should be our daily prayer namely, "lead me not into temptation." God will answer that prayer if sincerely prayed and if we do stumble into temptation, He stands ready to provide an escape for us.

F. *Pray for wisdom*—The Bible places a high value on wisdom. Pray to God for it and he will answer you (see James 1:5). God has promised and it will make life so much easier if we obtain wisdom.

G. *Be good Christian citizens*—I believe Christians have a responsibility to be good citizens of the country God has given us. That means taking part in social and political affairs using our faith and truth as we know it to vote and influence issues as we understand them. Vote for people and on issues that reflect biblical truth and guidance because that is the best way our nation can succeed and be the bright light on the hill that our world so desperately needs.

Let me close this section with some words from Dr. Charles F. Stanley, a wonderful Bible teacher, he says in his In Touch Bible readings for February 9, 2022 the following: "Your choices affect the direction of your life, so carefully consider what the Lord would have you to do. Scripture is clear that we perceive dimly (I Corinthians 13:12) but God sees the whole picture. That's why it's vital to rely upon His wisdom, truth, and directions in making decisions."

We can have access to God's will through prayer, Bible reading, and sensitivity to the leading of the Holy Spirit which God imparts to all believers. If perchance someone reading this is not a born-again Christian you can pray the Sinner's Prayer below and become a Christian if you pray it in sincerity. So, get on your knees and pray as follows:

> ***Dear God in heaven, I come to you in the name of Jesus. I acknowledge to you I am a sinner. I need and ask your forgiveness for the life I have led. I believe your only begotten son Jesus shed his precious blood on the cross of calvary and died for my sins. I believe he arose on the third day. I confess Jesus as my Lord and savior and dedicate my life henceforth to serving him. Amen***

If you prayed that prayer you are saved! Praise God! Congratulations and welcome to the church of Christ. Here's what you should do to follow up.

1. Find a good Bible believing church and fellowship with other children of God. You'll be spending eternity with them so get to know them.
2. Find a good daily devotional and start each day in brief fellowship with your God. Read a portion of scripture and pray to your God. It's the best way to start your day.
3. Look for God to open doors where your God given gifts might be used in his service in your church or community.
4. Get in the habit of praying to God regularly. Talk with him daily.

Other Book Titles From Dr. Harvey

1. 701 Sentence Sermons. (Grand Rapids, Michigan: Kregel Publications, 2000)
2. 701 More Sentence Sermons. (Grand Rapids, Michigan: Kregel Publications, 2002)
3. 701 Sentence Sermons – Vol. 3 (Grand Rapids, Michigan: Kregel Publications, 2005)
4. 701 Sentence Sermons – Vol. 4 (Grand Rapids, Michigan: Kregel Publications, 2007)
5. Every Day is Saturday (with Jackie Harvey). (St. Louis, Missouri: Concordia Publishing House, 2000) (Limited availability)
6. Does God Laugh? (Traverse City, Michigan: Harvest Day Books, 2008)
7. The Resurrection – Ruse or Reality? (Rapid City, South Dakota: CrossLink Publishing, 2011)
8. Letters from Perverse University. (Lincoln, Nebraska: Author's Press, 2001)
9. Seven for Heaven. (Lima, Ohio: CSS Publishing Co., 2003)
10. Run Thru the Tape. (Rapid City, South Dakota: CrossLink Publishing, 2009)
11. 1001 Sentence Sermons. (Tustin, California: Trilogy Christian Publishers, a wholly owned subsidiary of Trinity Broadcasting Network, 2021)
12. Does God Laugh? – Expanded Edition. (Tustin, California: Trilogy Christian Publishers, a wholly owned subsidiary of Trinity Broadcasting Network. 2021}

Index

A

Abortion 27, 28, 31, 33, 76, 83, 135, 199, 211
ACLU (American Civil Liberties Union) 52, 87, 115, 197
ADF (Alliance Defending Freedom) 202, 203
AFA (American Family Association) 17
Afghanistan 5, 206, 216
Allah 50, 179
Alliance 75, 120, 202
American 3, 5, 6, 14, 17, 22, 24, 26, 30, 31, 32, 33, 34, 39, 40, 41, 43, 46, 48, 54, 58, 59, 61, 62, 63, 69, 70, 75, 79, 83, 86, 88, 89, 91, 92, 93, 94, 95, 97, 100, 103, 104, 106, 108, 109, 112, 115, 120, 121, 122, 127, 128, 130, 131, 134, 136, 137, 139, 140, 143, 146, 147, 150, 152, 160, 169, 170, 172, 173, 175, 176, 177, 181, 186, 190, 191, 204, 205, 206, 212, 213, 214, 215, 221
Antifa 62, 63, 124, 136, 211
Antisemitism 56
APA (American Psychological Association) 130, 131, 132
Armageddon 224

B

Baptist 157
Barna Group 186
Behe, Michael 22
Bell, Derrick 176
Betrayal 120, 226, 227
Bible xiii, xiv, xv, xix, 15, 19, 24, 44, 52, 126, 127, 128, 152, 156, 159, 161, 178, 179, 184, 210, 224, 225, 226, 227, 230, 231, 232
Biden, Hunter 65, 66, 67, 177, 206, 211
Biden, Joe 65, 66, 67, 177, 206, 211
Bill of Rights 155
Bisexual 91, 100, 101
Blacks 47, 69, 70, 79, 105, 106, 111, 133, 134, 135, 141, 146, 147
BLM (Black Lives Matter) 62, 136, 137, 139
Border 213, 214, 215, 216
Boston 54
Breyer, Stephen 153, 211
Bureaucracy 40, 41, 138, 196

C

California 28, 29, 31, 36, 57, 72, 80, 124, 128
Carlson, Tucker 170
Carson, Ben 172
Catholic 31, 33, 97, 118, 127, 128, 161, 174, 184

CCP (Chinese Communist Party) 213
Censorship 123
Chamber of Commerce 216
Charter Schools 13, 172, 173
Chicago 35, 57, 134
China 3, 5, 205, 206, 208, 213, 219
Chinese xv, 3, 67, 213
Christianity xiii, 8, 10, 24, 52, 75, 76, 80, 82, 118, 128, 153, 155, 157, 164, 178, 179, 182, 197
Christians xvi, 13, 14, 24, 25, 31, 32, 33, 44, 49, 50, 51, 57, 76, 80, 83, 90, 98, 100, 101, 105, 115, 119, 124, 126, 135, 137, 150, 152, 153, 156, 158, 161, 179, 197, 202, 210, 223, 227, 229, 230, 231
CIA (Central Intelligence Agency) 209
Climate 1
Clinton, Bill 14
Colorado Civil Rights Commission 153, 202
Congressional 54, 56, 76, 94, 95
Constitution 24, 27, 32, 51, 58
Corinthians, Book of xiv, 193, 227, 228, 231
CRT (Critical Race Theory) 79, 112, 175, 176, 177, 208, 210, 211
Cuba v, 205, 208

D

Darwin, Charles 21
Debt 4, 5, 6, 25, 41, 42, 53, 54, 92, 94, 104, 128, 129, 163, 167, 168, 189, 204, 205, 206, 216, 222, 223
Deception viii, ix, xix, xx, 1, 4, 8, 12, 15, 18, 21, 24, 27, 30, 34, 37, 40, 43, 45, 46, 48, 49, 53, 56, 59, 62, 65, 69, 72, 75, 78, 82, 85, 88, 91, 94, 97, 100, 103, 107, 111, 114, 117, 120, 123, 126, 130, 133, 136, 140, 143, 146, 149, 152, 155, 157, 158, 162, 166, 169, 172, 175, 178, 181, 183, 186, 189, 190, 192, 195, 198, 201, 204, 208, 212, 215, 218, 221
Democrats 6, 28, 30, 31, 32, 56, 75, 76, 77, 105, 133, 134, 138, 141, 163, 182, 190, 206, 216, 219, 223
Denmark 51, 118
DeSantis, Ron 215
Devil xiii, xiv, xv, 18, 19, 20, 226, 228
DeVos, Betsy 13, 172
Dhimmis 50
Diversity 25, 78, 79, 80, 81, 108, 110
Divine, Miranda 177
Drucker, Peter 40
Dualism xiii
Durant, Ariel xiii, xvii
Durant, Will xiii, xvii

E

Easter 20, 181
E.L.C.A. (Evangelical Lutheran Church in America) 127, 164, 183
Enemy xv, xx, xxi, 3, 7, 12, 13, 14, 15, 16, 17, 21, 22, 23, 25, 26, 27, 28, 32, 34, 41, 42, 43, 44, 47, 51, 52, 58, 59, 60, 63, 64, 70, 77, 78, 79, 82, 83, 84, 89, 90, 91, 93, 97, 101, 103, 112, 114, 115, 119, 123, 124, 125, 126, 131, 133, 135, 136, 137, 138, 143, 144, 145, 147, 149, 151, 153, 158, 159, 160, 161, 162, 163, 164, 168,

175, 176, 179, 181, 182, 184, 187, 192, 193, 197, 200, 202, 209, 210, 214, 219, 220, 223
England 1, 35, 51, 104, 157, 161
English xiii, 85, 86, 87, 112, 149
Ephesians, Book of xiii
Episcopalians 164
Euphemism viii, 43
Evangelical 13, 45, 79, 127, 137
Evolution 21, 22, 24, 44, 83, 164

F

Family 8, 15, 17, 26, 38, 46, 48, 59, 66, 92, 102, 128, 130, 131, 132, 136, 143, 149, 150, 187, 206, 222, 223
F.B.I. (Federal Bureau of Investigation) 65, 177, 209, 210
Federal 4, 5, 9, 41, 54, 86, 93, 167, 205, 210, 222
Feminization 143
Flag 61, 69, 70, 78, 146, 147
Flower 201, 202
Fluke, Sandra 97
France 22, 35, 51
Freedom xvi, 10, 13, 24, 25, 80, 98, 104, 105, 124, 125, 131, 134, 155, 156, 201, 202, 209, 225, 226

G

Gallup 102, 161
Gandhi, Mahatma 162
Garland, Merrick 65, 67
Gays 38, 48, 76, 79, 100, 101, 107, 108, 109, 115, 127, 130, 151, 152, 179, 197, 199, 223
Gender vii, 15, 144
Generation 24, 25, 26, 60, 61, 77, 88, 114, 117, 121, 124, 137, 187, 222
Germany 51, 84, 208
Gibbons, Edward 167
Giuliani, Rudy 67
Gluttony 90, 187, 223
God xiii, xiv, xvi, 10, 19, 30, 31, 32, 38, 50, 57, 138, 179, 182, 184, 224, 225, 226, 227, 228, 229, 230, 231, 232
Gore, Al 1

H

Hannity, Shawn 170
Harris, Kamala 206
Harvey, Paul 18, 20
Higher Education 24
Hillsdale College 169
Hindus 31, 156
Hi-tech 88, 198, 200
HIV/Aids 44, 199
Holland 51
Horowitz, David 11, 103
House of Representatives 31, 32, 33, 57, 206
Hybels, Bill 179

I

Immorality 45, 46, 97, 98, 107, 150, 192, 198, 218
Infidels 49, 50, 57, 76
Inflategate 4
Iron triangle 189, 190
Isaiah xiii
Islam 38, 49, 50, 51, 52, 58, 76

J

James. Book of 229
Jefferson, Thomas 70, 147, 157
Jerusalem 30
Jewish 34, 56, 57, 58
John, Book of 224, 226
Judeo/Christian xvii, xix

K

Kavanaugh, Brett 27, 128
Kennedy, Anthony 192, 193
Killing 31, 44, 76, 84, 94, 126, 135, 172, 193, 216
Koran 31, 49, 50, 51, 52, 57, 76

L

Laziness 218
Left 1, 2, 5, 22, 33, 73, 74, 103, 109, 137, 138, 153, 155, 158, 164, 175, 206, 223
Levin, Mark 170
Lewis, C.S. xiii, xiv, xvi, xvii
LGBTQ 15, 24, 25, 32, 64, 73, 76, 79, 101, 128, 144, 153, 164, 202
Liberals 43, 74, 79, 118
Lincoln, Abe 39
Lindell, Mike 206
Los Angeles 35, 112
Loudounism 175, 176
Lucifer xiii, xv
Lukewarmness 26, 83, 161

M

Madison, James 70, 147
Mark, Book of 224, 227
Matthew, Book of 227
McConnell, Mitch 4

Media 19, 42, 43, 65, 75, 97, 98, 123, 124, 125, 140, 160, 169, 187, 191, 230
Michigan 31, 36, 56, 76, 129, 207
Military 5, 107, 109, 121, 222
Millennials 114, 123
Mohammed 50
Muslims 49, 50, 51, 56, 75, 76

N

NAMBLA (North American man/boy love association) 150
New York xvii, 1, 2, 11, 31, 36, 57, 81, 104, 169, 216
Nineth Circuit Court 29, 127
Nixon, Richard 2, 5

O

Obama, Barack 6, 8, 9, 10, 49, 53, 54, 97, 144, 167, 182, 204
Obesity 88, 89, 90
Ocasio-Cortes, Alexandria 137
Omar. Ilham 31, 56, 76

P

Pelosi, Nancy 33
Pentagon 5, 109, 121, 144
Pentecostals 184
Pew Research 137
Planned Parenthood 28
Pope 33
Pornography 19, 44, 46, 47, 60, 127, 128, 160, 164, 167, 187, 199, 229
Portland, (Oregon) 139
Postscript 224
Prager, Dennis 37
Presbyterians 164, 183

P.U. (Perverse University) xix, 4, 6, 8, 14, 18, 22, 47, 51, 53, 69, 82, 85, 88, 89, 115, 126, 139, 146, 150, 155, 158, 160, 162, 166, 183, 187, 213

R

Racism 9, 32, 79, 103, 174, 175, 177, 211
Reid, Harry 182
Republicans 4, 28, 56, 67, 75, 76, 98, 105, 109, 134, 138, 140, 141, 176, 206, 214, 216, 217
Revelations, Book of 82, 224
Robes 192, 194
Rome 107, 168, 218, 221, 222
Roosevelt, F.D. 9, 122, 190
Russia 5, 121, 208

S

San Francisco, (California) xv, 57, 69, 146
Satan xiii, xiv, xv, xvi, xix, xxi, 3, 8, 10, 11, 12, 15, 17, 18, 21, 22, 24, 25, 26, 27, 28, 30, 34, 43, 49, 52, 55, 59, 63, 64, 65, 67, 77, 78, 83, 89, 98, 101, 110, 120, 122, 126, 127, 138, 139, 141, 142, 143, 149, 152, 153, 155, 156, 157, 158, 159, 160, 162, 166, 167, 168, 170, 173, 174, 176, 177, 179, 181, 184, 189, 190, 191, 192, 193, 194, 195, 200, 201, 203, 204, 206, 207, 208, 213, 216, 218, 219, 221, 222, 223, 225, 226, 227, 228, 229, 230
Savage, Michael 60, 170

Schumer, Chuck 4, 6, 33
Secularism 117, 155, 156
Senate 28, 31, 33, 95, 134, 217
Sharia Law 51, 57, 58, 75, 76
Sixteen Nineteen (1619 Project) 103
Social justice 25, 79
Solomon 179, 183, 184
Soros, George 34, 35, 36, 74, 124, 138, 209
Speech 25, 44, 46, 61, 72, 73, 74, 76, 80, 93, 124, 125, 131, 204, 209
Spong, John Shelby 128, 178
Stanley, Charles 231
St. Louis, (Missouri) 35
Stutzman, Baronelle 201, 202
Suicide xv, 168, 195
Supreme Court (SCOTUS) 27, 46, 91, 115, 127, 128, 131, 135, 152, 153, 156, 192, 201, 206, 209
Sura 49, 50, 57
Sweden 51, 84, 118, 178, 179

T

Tainter, Joseph 195, 196
Talib, Rashida 31, 56
Tax 13, 41, 48, 50, 54, 80, 98, 108, 170, 173
Temptation 187, 228, 231
Ten Commandments 24, 60, 126, 127, 156
Thessalonians, Book of 219
Tournier, Paul xiv, xvi, xvii, 225
Triangle 189, 190
Trillion 4, 6, 25, 41, 54, 92, 94, 163, 167, 204, 205, 206, 223
Trump, Donald 3, 6, 12, 53, 54, 76, 131, 133, 135, 140, 159, 169, 170, 172

U

UCC, (United Church of Christ) 101
Ukraine 67
UMC, (United Methodist Church) 183

V

Values xvii, xx, 1, 4, 7, 8, 10, 12, 13, 15, 16, 18, 21, 24, 25, 26, 27, 30, 31, 32, 34, 37, 39, 40, 43, 46, 49, 53, 56, 59, 62, 63, 65, 69, 70, 71, 72, 75, 77, 78, 82, 85, 88, 91, 92, 93, 94, 97, 100, 101, 103, 107, 111, 114, 117, 118, 120, 122, 123, 126, 127, 130, 133, 136, 137, 140, 143, 146, 147, 149, 152, 153, 155, 156, 157, 162, 166, 168, 169, 172, 173, 175, 176, 178, 181, 183, 186, 187, 189, 192, 195, 197, 198, 199, 201, 202, 204, 208, 212, 215, 218, 221, 226

Vatican 9
Venezuela 205, 208
View xiv, xv, 47, 72, 164, 199, 223
Voucher 172, 173, 174

W

Warren, Rick 179
Washington, D.C. 57, 62
Washington, George 32, 70, 139, 147, 155
Wokism v, 175
World xiii, xiv, xv, xvii, xix, 2, 3, 18, 22, 35, 41, 56, 57, 63, 70, 76, 81, 92, 97, 105, 118, 121, 138, 147, 162, 164, 173, 174, 190, 196, 205, 206, 208, 219, 223, 231
Wray, Christopher 65, 67

Z

Zimbabwe 205, 208

www.ingramcontent.com/pod-product-compliance
Lightning Source LLC
LaVergne TN
LVHW011936070526
838202LV00054B/4668